Praise for Sami Lee's
Sunset Knight

"...A beautiful, erotic tale of love overcoming obstacles. I absolutely loved this book! It was exciting and touching. The characters are wonderful... The sex scenes are very hot, and kinky. But in each one you can see the trust building and love growing... The emotions were so well written. During some of the scenes where Lana is going through her heartache, my eyes actually watered. Now that is pulling you into the story."

~ *The Romance Studio*

"...The characters quite literally pop off the page, each one as well developed as the one before... Sunset Knight is one for the keeper shelf that I highly recommend. If you like a heaping portion of romance in your erotica, this definitely hits the spot."

~ *Whipped Cream Reviews*

"Ms. Lee takes us right into the guts of the relationship between Lana and Brody. Delving deep into what makes Brody the man he is, we're treated to a real look at real people who appear to be polar opposites making it work... Sunset Knight delivers a roller coaster ride of emotions well worth reading."

~ *Fallen Angel Reviews*

"This is just plain delicious and captivating until the very end!"

~ *Book Junkie*

Look for these titles by
Sami Lee

Now Available:

Born Again Virgin
Fijian Fling
Chasing Sunset

Print Anthology
Midsummer Night's Steam: Sand, Sun and Sex

Sunset Knight

Sami Lee

A SAMHAIN PUBLISHING, LTD. publication.

Samhain Publishing, Ltd.
577 Mulberry Street, Suite 1520
Macon, GA 31201
www.samhainpublishing.com

Sunset Knight
Copyright © 2010 by Sami Lee
Print ISBN: 978-1-60504-820-8
Digital ISBN: 978-1-60504-689-1

Editing by Anne Scott
Cover by Mandy M. Roth

First Samhain Publishing, Ltd. electronic publication: November 2009
First Samhain Publishing, Ltd. print publication: October 2010

Dedication

To the audacity of inexperience.

Many thanks to the Princess and the Cherub, for waiting time and again while Mummy wrote "one more page" of this book, author and friend Jess Dee for her impassioned opinions about the deficiencies of the original ending, and to my editor Anne for her faith in the polished product.

Chapter One

"You're not getting here until *Saturday*? What kind of best man rocks up the day before the groom's wedding?"

Brody Nash grinned as Drew Buchanan's incredulous words barked at him through his mobile phone and replied, "The kind who warned you he wasn't suddenly going to turn into Mr. Reliable just because you're whipped."

"Whipped and loving it." Brody could hear the happiness in his old friend's voice as he referred to his fiancée. "You ought to try it. God knows no one needs to be pulled into line more than you."

"She'd have to be seven foot tall and armed."

"Nah—I reckon short and sassy would do it."

There was an awkward silence into which they both inserted the obvious—*like Sidney*. About six months ago Brody had thought exactly along those lines, which had landed him in an ill-advised three way and at the wrong end of Drew's fist. Brody's infatuation with his best friend's girl had almost destroyed his relationship with Drew, but as usual Buchanan hadn't given up on him when he probably should have. Story of their lives.

"The weekend is the best I can do," Brody said as he approached the back entrance of Drew's restaurant, the Blue Fish Grill. He figured Drew would be in the process of closing up for the night, and the likelihood that he'd scream like a girl when Brody snuck up on him was pleasingly high. "I don't control the northerly winds."

"Northerly winds," Drew scoffed. "More likely you got sidetracked. Which was it this time, blonde or brunette?"

"Redhead, actually." Brody frowned, wondering why he lied. He hadn't hooked up with a woman in the past week, or in the past six months in fact, an anomaly in terms of his usual pattern. The drought wasn't due to a lack of opportunity, but more to a sense of restlessness that he didn't think could be cured by mindless sex. The idea of losing himself in the temporary heat of a woman he barely knew and would soon forget had actually bored him.

"You're a piece of work, Nash. You'd better be here on time. Rufus is my second choice for best man and he isn't even house trained. I'm not sure he's up to wearing a tux."

Rufus was a big, hairy mixed-breed puppy Brody had read about via email. From what he'd heard, Sidney treated that mutt like a newborn baby, which Brody figured was next on her list of must-haves. Buchanan really was going all out at this commitment thing. "It's nice to know my backup is a mongrel. Is this a comment on my skills as a best man or my sparkling personality?"

"Take it as you like. Just be here before the wedding or Sidney's going to have my ass."

"Doesn't sound like hard labor to me."

"Watch yourself, Nash. That's my future wife you're talking about."

Brody winced at the icy edge in his friend's voice. "Sorry, man. Too soon?"

Relief seeped through him at Drew's chuckle. "Nah, it's all right. I can afford to be generous. Winners are grinners."

Brody laughed at Drew's smug tone. There had never been any real competition when it came to winning Sidney's affections, and Brody had stopped wasting time on "perhaps if I'd met her first" conjectures. For one, he was glad Drew was happy. Secondly, if he'd met Sidney first, he would have fucked up her life. So all things considered everything turned out as it should have.

Pushing open the unlocked back door, Brody stealthily crossed the kitchen and peered into the restaurant's dining area. He saw a woman gyrating to a raunchy number blaring from the stereo system—something about getting dirty that he vaguely recognized—while simultaneously running a broom over the polished wood floorboards. Her ponytail shone a deep russet in the sparse restaurant lighting as she spun it around to the melody, her narrow hips swinging in time to the pounding beat. A redhead. And a hot one at that.

"Nash, is that Christina Aguilera?"

"Who?" The woman had just started dancing around the broomstick and using it as a microphone. Amused and more than a little intrigued, Brody watched the sinuous silhouette of her body move against the backdrop of the marina and the few lights of Graceville's main street beyond.

"Either your musical tastes have changed markedly or that's Sid's CD playing in the background. You're at the restaurant, aren't you?"

Brody made some noise of assent and listened with half an ear while Drew read him the riot act for pulling his leg about not being able to make it back for days yet. Drew's new waitress had an absolutely phenomenal pair of long, slender legs and she knew how to use them. Brody let his gaze trail over her until it came to rest on her stocking feet where they slid across the floor.

The song ended and the silence that came after throbbed. The girl heaved a sigh and bowed toward the empty restaurant. "Thank you, thank you," she said. "You've been a wonderful audience."

"You're welcome."

She spun around and shrieked. She dropped the broom and her feet got tangled in the handle. There was a loud thud as she tripped and landed on the hardwood floor. "Ooouch!"

"What the hell was that?"

Into the phone Brody explained, "I think I just scared the shit out of the new waitress. I thought it was you locking up."

Another song came blaring out of the stereo, a ballad this time. Brody had trouble hearing Drew's words so he turned the volume down before striding toward the woman on the floor and offering his hand.

She eyed his outstretched arm as though it were a venomous snake. Brody's attention was arrested by the fascinating hues fanning out from the dark spots of her pupils—multifacets of gold, treacle and honey contained within almond-shaped eyes that turned up just a little at the outer edges. A spark of recognition flared.

But the girl she reminded Brody of wore glasses and wasn't a redhead. Neither did Lana Green wear her skirts so satisfactorily short. This couldn't be her.

"Courtney's the only new waitress I've hired in the past six months, and she's not on tonight," Drew said as, finally, the girl on the floor slipped her hand into Brody's. She had slim fingers, strong yet ladylike. The short, practical nails were tipped with a pearlescent pink polish. Brody drew her to her feet easily. For a tall woman she weighed next to nothing. When he tugged on her hand her slender body came barreling into his.

They stood there, chest to chest. Brody's nose rested close

to that jaunty ponytail and the scent of apples and cinnamon teased his nostrils. He heard Drew's words—*it must be Lana*—as though from far away, and he had to question if he'd misunderstood. Lana Green had worked at the Grill for three years. Brody would have noticed if she'd had such ogle-worthy legs.

But those eyes...

Wanting to see them again, Brody pulled back a little. He looked into an oval-shaped face with wide, lightly glossed lips and a nose that was perhaps a little too long to be classically pretty. His mind's eye took away the subtle flattery of makeup and added a pair of wire-framed glasses. "Lana?"

She opened her mouth as if to say something. All that came out was a soft puff of breath that tickled through the hair on his chin, reminding him of the beard he'd grown purely out of neglect. Maybe she still hadn't recognized *him*. Wearing the ratty clothes he'd sailed his yacht, the *Sunset*, back to Graceville in, he probably looked like a homeless guy who'd broken in to rob the till.

"I didn't mean to scare you." He would never have crept up on her if he'd known she was locking up alone. "It's Brody."

"I know who you are." Lana gave him an incredulous look. "Didn't you know who I was?"

Well, now she'd made him feel like a real dope about it. "You look different."

"It wouldn't hurt to tell her she looks nice, Nash." Brody frowned at Drew's remonstrance. How had he forgotten he was still holding the mobile phone to his ear? "Try and keep the staff happy. You'll have to be a little more personable when you take over."

"Yeah, yeah." More personable his butt. He'd have to get a full-blown personality transplant if he wanted to keep everyone as happy as Drew seemed to do with minimal effort. Brody had agreed to fill in as the Grill's manager while Drew was on his honeymoon, but he hoped his friend didn't expect flawless results. The food was his thing—people were not.

Belatedly, Brody became aware he was still resting a hand against the soft indent of Lana's waist. Probably why there was a hint of uneasiness in her eyes. Releasing her, he took a step back. He must have moved too abruptly because the sudden loss of his support seemed to unbalance her. She stumbled backward, her feet coming in contact with the fallen broom handle again. For the second time in as many minutes, she tripped and landed on the floor with a resounding thump.

"Ooouch!"

"Jesus, what are you doing to that girl?"

Brody scowled, feeing as disorientated as Lana appeared. "Nothing," he told Drew a little defensively. It wasn't his fault Lana was a klutz. She always seemed to be tripping over something. "Listen, why don't I come by in the morning? You can measure me up for a penguin suit."

"All right, see you then. Hey, can I talk to Lana for a sec?"

"Hang on." She was still sitting on the floor, resting her head on her bent knees. Brody crouched beside her. "Are you okay?"

She nodded without lifting her head. Brody wondered if she was in serious pain and if she might be about to cry. Anxiety sliced through him. He hated it when women cried. Made him feel helpless and ineffectual every time. "You sure?"

At last she raised her gaze to his, her expression more embarrassed than distressed. "Nothing that an ice pack to the butt wouldn't fix."

Brody's lips twitched. He barely managed to refrain from offering to help her with that as he handed the phone over.

"Drew wants to talk to you."

Taking the device, she pressed it to her ear. "Hey, Drew."

A smile curved her lips as she started giving Drew a rundown of how the end of the night had gone. The wariness that had been in her expression when she'd faced Brody cleared as she spoke to Drew, shared a laugh with him. The obvious change in her demeanor irritated Brody for some reason.

Lana tried to push herself to her feet. Brody noticed she gave a little wince when she rested her weight on her ankle and instinct came out of nowhere. He slipped an arm beneath her bent knees, another around her shoulders and stood, hoisting her against him.

She let out a gasp and grew utterly still in his arms, every muscle in her body tense as he carried her into the kitchen. That hint of spicy apple hit him again, made him think of hot pie fresh from the oven and the girl next door a troublemaker like him would never be allowed to touch.

Not that he wanted to touch her. He carried her out of pure necessity.

He set her carefully on the stainless-steel counter, aware of what she'd said about her butt needing an ice pack. For the purposes of first aid—definitely not because the idea of touching her appealed in any way—Brody lifted her foot and examined it. He pressed his fingers into the flesh around the point of her ankle, trying to figure out if there was any swelling.

There didn't appear to be. The only swelling in the room seemed to be in the region of his jockey shorts.

Lana's eyes shot to his and Brody abruptly dropped her foot. Could she tell he was getting aroused from doing nothing more than touching her leg? Christ. Six months was obviously too long to go without.

"He's still here," Lana said to Drew. Then her brow

furrowed, deep lines creasing the smooth skin. "That's not necessary, but if you insist, I'll tell him."

At last she clicked the disconnect button and handed back the phone. The second she faced him her expression seemed guarded, as though her defenses were once again engaged. It dawned on Brody what had been nagging him. She treated him differently than everyone else—always had. While she laughed and joked with Drew and the other guys who worked here, she'd never appeared that at ease in his presence. It was almost as if she was afraid of him. At the very least it seemed she disliked him.

So what? Brody asked himself. A lot of people didn't like him and he'd never wasted a minute thinking about it before.

Turning away, he stalked to the cool room. Inside he found some ice and bagged it, allowing the frigid air to quell his burgeoning erection. His annoyance over Lana's attitude mystified him. She was a nice girl, and he wasn't a very nice guy. It shouldn't have irked that she didn't like him. He could just imagine her reaction if he got her in bed and started doing some of the stuff he liked to do...

He wasn't going to get her into bed. It was bizarre that he would even have the thought.

Brody carried the makeshift cold pack out to where she sat. "What are you supposed to tell me?" His question came out sounding brusque. Was it any wonder she was wary of him?

"I'm in strife." She watched, her eyes doing that anxious thing again, as he lifted her foot and pressed the bag to her ankle. "I'm not supposed to lock up on my own but Mick wanted to catch a soccer match at O'Ryan's Pub and I told him to go ahead. Drew said you should stay until I finish, but you don't have to. You don't have to do that either." She gestured to where he was holding her foot. "I said I was fine."

"Preventative medicine." Brody supposed she was hinting that she didn't want him to stay. Apparently she'd feel safer taking her chances against potential vandals and thieves than with him. "And I'll stay. Drew's right, Mick shouldn't have taken off." Mick Jensen was a pretty good chef and a likeable enough guy but he did have a tendency toward forgetfulness and other lackadaisical behavior.

Her shoulders squared. "I told him I could handle things. Graceville's not exactly crime-spree city."

"The night's takings are in the safe, aren't they? A woman alone is asking for trouble."

She issued a delicate snort and muttered, sounding almost annoyed about it, "I've never asked for trouble in my life."

Brody caught her gaze and smiled. "It's not all it's cracked up to be."

Be personable, Drew had said. Try not to scare the crap out of this poor girl. Maybe, with a bit of effort, he could even make her like him a little. Just to grease the wheels at work, he told himself, as she was Drew's most experienced waitress. Not because he suddenly couldn't recall why celibacy had seemed like a realistic option for the past six months.

He wasn't going to break his drought with Lana Green, anyway. Playing where he worked was not something he did routinely. Or ever, if you didn't count Sidney and that whole fiasco.

Lana wriggled her toes, highlighting their proximity to his groin, and he had to stifle a groan. *No way.* Brody tamped down the surprising surge of desire with effort. Even he wasn't that stupid.

Although he resembled an escapee from a Mexican prison, Brody Nash looked good enough to eat. And his continued touch on her foot was making Lana a very hungry woman.

Calling on the skills she'd acquired from years of long practice, she did her best not to let it show how his nearness affected her. Maintaining an air of indifference was tremendously difficult because he'd never touched her like this before. He'd never touched her, period, at least not deliberately. And anytime they'd accidentally brushed up against each other in the course of a night's work, Lana had darted away as quickly as she could, lest he perceive that even unintentional contact with him set every nerve end in her body on fire.

While his gaze was concentrated on her ankle, Lana allowed herself the pleasure of studying him. He'd grown a beard that encircled his cynical lips in a way that drew attention to their sensual fullness. His hair was long, curling like black silk over his shirt collar. The T-shirt he wore was dark and rumpled, the cotton stretching over his shoulders and arms, emphasizing their broad strength.

He didn't look like a prisoner so much as a pirate, just returned from months at sea. Blackbeard seemed a fitting moniker. *Ravish any wenches lately, Brody?* If only he thought of her in that way, he would barely have to lift one of those dark sardonic brows and he could ravish her too.

If only.

"So what happened to the glasses?"

"What glasses?"

He glanced up and their gazes locked before Lana could prepare herself. Something flickered in the enigmatic depths of his eyes, turning them hot as fresh espresso. "Yours." He cleared his throat as though he had something caught in it. His expression turned bemused, the lilt of his lips teasing. "Your glasses."

Well *duh*. "I got struck by lightning and now I have perfect twenty-twenty vision." He looked at her as though he were trying to figure out if she had all her ducks in a row. "Sorry. I got contacts." When his focus passed over her ponytail she added, "And I dyed my hair. Did you really not recognize me before?"

"I told you." His assessing eyes wandered over her. Intense. Thorough. *Hot.* "You look different."

Whoa. Had she imagined that look? In addition to the contacts and new hairstyle, Lana had shortened her skirts and begun wearing a little makeup. She'd been told she had nice legs and she figured her eyes and mouth weren't bad, as features went. Her nose had a small bump in the bridge and she had more freckles than she would have liked, but she wasn't ugly. Lately, she'd been accentuating her few good points, instead of lamenting the many attractions she didn't possess. She hadn't thought for a minute the small changes she'd made would garner Brody's attention.

"I could say the same to you," she at last responded.

His rueful chuckle reverberated through her as he ran a hand over his thick beard. "Yeah, perhaps I ought to shave before I go see Sidney and Drew. Drew's already threatened to demote me from best man, and I'm told Rufus is eager to step in."

"You might have some competition there. Rufus can fetch sticks so wedding rings should be a piece of cake."

"I don't fetch. But I've never tried to hump anybody's leg either."

His droll retort renewed Lana's awareness that her foot was still resting quite comfortably on *his* leg. Or more specifically, his thigh. She could feel taut muscle against her toes, which were planted mere inches away from his fly. She couldn't prevent the way her attention snagged on that spot, or the lust that arrowed through her at the thought of any part of her body, even her pinkie toe, sharing proximity with *that* part of him.

It would be so easy to curve her leg around his hip and draw him toward her, until his chest was once again brushing against hers as it had when he'd lifted her from the floor. She could make some comment, some bawdy reference to *humping* and watch those dark eyes flare with surprise and, hopefully, interest.

It would be so easy. If she were somebody else. Someone with the courage to act on her impulses without fear of probable rejection. The kind of woman a man like Brody was attracted to and not some clumsy geek who lost all ability to coordinate her limbs around him. Tripping over that broom *twice* proved that whatever improvements she'd made to her appearance hadn't given her the confidence to be cool and collected with Brody in the room.

Lifting the ice pack from her flesh, he tossed it on the counter beside her and turned away so her foot dropped, the contact between them obliterated so fast it made Lana blink. "Your ankle looks fine."

"Told you."

"What else do you need help with?"

The help she needed ought to come from a trained psychologist. Or perhaps a hypnotist. There had to be a cure for the Brody Nash Obsession out there somewhere. A patch? Gum? Another man?

Lana had tried the last several times in the past five months since her parents had moved their dogmatic conservatism to a retirement villa on the Gold Coast and she had decided to get herself a sex life. So far, she hadn't found a candidate worthy, which was proving endlessly frustrating. Why was the only man she could see herself sleeping with the most unattainable man of all?

"Lana?"

Levering herself off the counter, she dropped to the floor. Other than the weakness in her knees that always seemed to plague her in Brody's presence, her legs were in full working order. "It's all done. I should get home to bed."

Brody's eyebrows hiked. "In a hurry?"

Was he asking if someone was waiting for her? She wished. "I have to get up early tomorrow. I work from home too." At his look she elucidated, "I build websites."

"Really?"

"Don't I look like a computer geek without my glasses?"

His gaze passed over her again, the way it had earlier. "You don't look like any kind of geek, with or without glasses."

Oh. My. God. Was he flirting? He was definitely staring at her like she was a woman, not some maladroit girl who wouldn't warrant his attention. Lana's heart accelerated, began pounding hard against her ribs. She knew his type of woman— beautiful, seductive, confident. In other words, the very antithesis of her. He must be amusing himself at her expense.

Lana felt transported back to high school, and the few times a cute boy had bothered to talk to her. Invariably, she discovered he did it on a dare, or that he was entertaining himself momentarily with the nerd so she'd help him with calculus.

"I have to go." She headed out to the restaurant and grabbed her stuff from the cupboard behind the bar, anger fuelling her strides. She felt Brody watching as she slipped on her shoes and backpack, and then grabbed her motorbike helmet.

"You ride?"

It probably wasn't the type of riding he thought, but Lana answered, "Yep."

"What sort?"

"A Yamaha."

"This I've gotta see. I'll walk you out."

Couldn't he tell she was mad at him? Arguing the point would only delay her departure further, so Lana remained silent as they left the restaurant and she used her keys to lock up. Their shoes crunched on the gravel as they traversed the car park, her low-heeled pumps making far less of an impression than Brody's heavy-soled shoes. At almost five ten, Lana wasn't petite, but the whole broad-shouldered, hard-muscled six feet of man at her side made her feel that way.

Brody started laughing before they were halfway to her mode of transportation. Lana pursed her lips. He wasn't the first to tease her about the scooter. "You never asked how many cc's it was."

"Do they use cc's for that thing or amps?"

"Very funny. Men always think size matters."

Brody's laughter petered out but the amusement still tinged his voice. "Sometimes it does."

The innuendo was unmistakable, and Lana felt herself flush. She supposed he was used to women well practiced in sexual banter, but she was nowhere near capable of it, not with him. "It's not very nice of you to tease me."

She could sense the surprise in his eyes as he slanted her a look. "Sor-*ry*. But it *is* a girlie bike."

Hardly able to tell him that wasn't the teasing she was referring to, Lana said, "I am a girl. Anyway, I like it. It gets me where I want to go." It sure beat the rust heap of a Toyota sedan that had finally died on her a few months ago, she thought, giving her blue Yamaha Bee Wee an admiring glance.

Lana pulled the band from her hair and shook out her ponytail before slipping the open-face helmet on and straddling the bike. She glanced up and found Brody's eyes trained on her, his expression hinting at a fascination she would never have thought herself capable of engendering in any man, let alone this one. Lana told herself to breathe. *Breathe in, breathe out.*

"I like your new look." His gaze roamed over her face slowly, at last connecting with hers. "It's a shame to hide eyes like that behind a pair of specs."

Nervous excitement gave way to anger, which sharpened to a hard, flinty point of hurt inside her. "You can't go around looking at women like that if you don't mean it—at least not at *me*. I'm not good at casual flirting, and I don't appreciate being made fun of."

He reared back as though her words had zapped him like electricity. "You think I'm making fun of you?"

"My eyes are brown, Brody. You're not interested in me, so please don't act like you are. It's cruel."

His brows scrunched as he stared at her. Lana had time to dimly sense that he was holding his breath, to realize she was holding hers, before his head dipped. His lips settled on hers and her pulse stilled, her body remaining motionless as his mouth mobilized, began to explore.

Heart fluttering, Lana tightened her grip on the scooter's handlebars. She wasn't game to reach out and touch him, to move even a millimeter, lest any action on her part break the spell. The moment she'd long ago given up dreaming about was actually happening. Brody Nash was kissing her.

His lips were warm and soft, the rasp of his beard against her chin a masculine sensation that had desire breaking out of its safe box and running free through her blood like salmon swimming upstream—instinctual, single-minded, ultimately doomed. Pragmatism told her he was still teasing her.

What if he wasn't?

A sigh escaped her mouth and pushed its way into his as Lana at last reacted. She parted her lips and invited the soft sweep of his tongue, lifted her hand and threaded it through his hair, pulling him closer. He drew in a sharp, surprised breath, his hand rising to cup her head. The contact sounded loud in Lana's ears as he bumped the helmet she wore.

He retreated abruptly. Stepping back, he swore, staring at her as though she'd sprouted a second head. Lana brought her hand to her lips. They felt singed where Brody's had been pressed against them a moment ago. "You kissed me."

He pushed out a breath, sounding as stunned as she did. "Yeah."

"Why?"

"I don't know. I've been at sea for six months."

"Oh, that's nice."

"I didn't mean that the way it sounded." He scratched a hand over his beard, appearing beleaguered. His gaze swept over her and once again she saw that look of astonishment flicker in his eyes. "You look really good tonight. I guess it threw me."

This was getting better and better. "Your surprise is so flattering."

"Hell, Lana. You're a pretty girl, I didn't mean to imply you weren't." Lana resisted the urge to insist she was a woman not a girl. Debating the point would only make her look petulant. "Drew told me to be nice to you, and I was only trying to do that," he explained in a mutter. "But I don't think this is what he had in mind."

"Drew told you to be nice to me?"

"You and the rest of the staff. Somehow I've got to try and fill his shoes for a couple of weeks."

"And you're planning on kissing everyone to achieve that aim? The girls might like it but I'm not so sure Mick and the apprentices would take it well."

His gaze dropped to her mouth. "You liked it?"

Lana's pulse picked up speed again. His body inclined toward her, as though he was considering giving a follow-up performance if she vacillated on the issue. Much as the notion appealed it also piqued her temper. She couldn't believe he thought she would let him kiss her again after the insulting way he'd tried to explain away his actions.

Well, she probably would. Of course she would. His kiss had had a potent margarita effect—smooth and delicious, with a pleasing salty aftertaste and a mean kick that made her thirst for seconds. But he needn't know that, the arrogant swine. She lifted her shoulders in a careless shrug. "It was fine."

"It was *fine*?"

Lana almost laughed at the look on his face. This was some turnaround, making him feel inadequate for a change. She shrugged again, letting him assume she'd had better when in reality nothing in her past had come close to the thrill of that kiss. "You don't have to worry I'm going to tell Drew, or make things difficult at work because you kissed me. Apparently it was an accident," she added in a drawl. "And as for being in charge—maybe you should do things your own way. You're not Drew, so just be yourself."

"Be myself." His lips quirked. "You've known me three years, Lana. You really think that's the answer?"

"What are you afraid of—that someone might find out who you really are?"

She saw she'd gone too far when his smile slid away and his eyes shuttered. He straightened and the cool bay breeze swept into the breach that widened between them. "You're the one who ought to be scared, of doing yourself an injury on that thing. Ride carefully, will ya?"

Inwardly cursing herself for putting an end to the longest conversation she'd ever had with Brody, Lana turned on the ignition. Some of his amusement resurfaced at the tinny sound of the engine chortling gaily to life. She raised her voice over the noise. "I'll have you know I've been riding the Bee Wee for three months, and I haven't had a bingle yet."

"Three months," he grumbled. "You're a novice."

At more things than riding, Lana thought, relieved he didn't know the truth. A virgin at twenty-three—it was darned embarrassing. She wondered if Brody would laugh if he found out.

She thought of the only way in which he could discover the fact and flushed hot all over. Maybe it would be worth the humiliation.

Not that she'd ever considered Brody would want to do the deflowering honors. But then, she'd never thought he'd turn around and notice she wasn't the same awkward geek she'd been three years ago, and tonight it seemed he'd done just that. He'd talked and touched, flirted and kissed, more progress in half an hour than Lana had made in three years of secret pining. Accident or not, a kiss was still a kiss. It had to mean *something*. There was always a chance that Brody would have another lip-locking mishap, especially if she found the right way to encourage him.

As she eased the scooter out of its parking space and

headed for the turnoff to Main Street, Lana smiled to herself. Anticipation expanded inside her like a helium-filled balloon, making her feel lighter and lighter as she got closer to home. Her life had definitely taken a turn into interesting territory.

Chapter Two

The bride was late.

Only by fifteen minutes, which Lana figured was understandable given all a woman had to do to prepare for a wedding. By the look on the groom's face as he glanced at his watch for the umpteenth time, she didn't think he shared the same understanding.

"She wouldn't stand him up, would she?"

Lana sent a sideways glance toward Courtney Fitzsimmons. "No way."

"Marriage is a huge deal. Maybe she chickened out."

"Nothing's going to stop Sidney getting here—she's nuts about Drew."

"Oh my God," Courtney groaned. "You believe in true love, don't you?"

"Why not? Don't you?"

The brunette's lips twisted bitterly. "Not lately. Tony and I broke up."

"Oh no." Lana tried to remember how long Courtney had been dating Tony. Courtney had only been working at the Blue Fish Grill a few months and already there'd been a Tony, a Simon, a Ryan and she thought a Brian. Lana wasn't entirely sure those last two weren't the same guy and she'd misheard the name. "I'm sorry to hear that."

"Don't be sorry. Turns out he wanted to post naked pictures of me on some website called Horny Housewives dot com."

"How awful!"

"Tell me about it. Do you think I look old enough to be a housewife? My ass I do."

A woman sitting in the row in front of them turned and displayed a filthy look, to which Courtney responded with a suitably chastened expression. They settled into guilty quiet again while the small crowd of invited guests began to shift uncomfortably in their white fold-out chairs.

The heat of the balmy Sunday afternoon was ameliorated by the ample shade cast by the arbor above them. Blooming wisteria draped from its framework, imbuing the air with a sweet fragrance that mingled pleasantly with the salty breeze drifting in from the Pacific. Lana surveyed the crowd idly, a ruse to cover the true focus of her attention, who was standing at the altar beside the groom.

Doing his Blackbeard impersonation the other night, Brody had looked gorgeous. Clean shaven, wearing a formal suit with his hair freshly trimmed, he was beyond delicious. As she watched from the fourth row, Brody leaned forward and said something to Drew, who was once again dragging his hand through his tawny hair and pointing to his watch. Taking advantage of the other man's closeness, Brody grabbed Drew's wrist and snatched the watch from it, slipping it into his suit pocket.

Lana smothered a grin. As though he sensed her amusement, Brody's gaze scanned the small gathering until it collided with hers. Seeing the mirth on her face, he responded to it with a half smile that made her heart trip over.

"The best man's a dish." Courtney's statement mirrored Lana's thoughts. "Who is he?"

"That's Brody. He's going to be filling in for Drew while he's away."

"Really?" Courtney asked with interest.

"Forget it, Courtney." On Courtney's opposite side, Mick Jensen joined in the conversation. "Brody's a shark—eats women alive and moves on. Wouldn't you rather date a nice guy, someone you could cuddle up to at night?"

At the suggestive way Mick waggled his blond eyebrows, Courtney shoved at his shoulder. "Come off it, Mick. I'm not that desperate."

"Ouch." Mick settled a hand over his chest. "My poor wounded heart."

"You'll survive. Some girls might like this whole *look* you have going." Courtney gestured at Mick's dress slacks and vibrant purple and blue paisley shirt. It wasn't an outfit many guys could carry off, but in Lana's opinion Mick had such a jovial way about him his odd sense of style hardly mattered.

Yet Courtney sniffed in distaste. "Look at you, you're like a cockney David Spade."

"I wish I was." Mick tossed his longish blond hair out of his cheeky baby blues and ramped up his British accent. "I could make me a million quid acting like a dweeb."

"And here you are, doing it for free."

"Could we call a truce today, guys?" Lana entreated with a long-suffering sigh. "This is a happy occasion."

"Spoken like a true romantic," Courtney drawled. "Wait a few years, Lana, and that optimism will wear off."

"We're the same age."

"Yeah, but something tells me I've got more miles on my

speedometer."

Mick leaned in close and whispered, "Any time you want to rack up a few extra, I'm available."

Courtney sent her spike heel careening into his leg, making Mick wince. "One day I'm going to give up on you, Court. How will you feel then?"

"Like I don't have to get that restraining order after all."

Mick muttered, "I know when I'm not welcome," before turning back to Jack, the young guy who worked as a bartender at the restaurant.

"Doesn't seem like he knows squat," Courtney said to Lana.

"Mick's not so bad. I think he's quite sweet."

"You can have him."

Lana laughed. "It's not that way with us. We're friends."

Courtney narrowed her green eyes shrewdly. "So who did we get all dressed up for then?"

Lana glanced down at herself, running her palms over the smooth fabric of her purple silk shift dress. The thin straps and crossover empire style top showed off a lot more skin than she usually dared to, and while she could easily have gotten away without wearing a bra, she'd worn a strapless one underneath the dress because the padding gave her at least the illusion of cleavage. "I look all right?"

"Oh yeah. If I didn't know better I'd say you were hoping to get lucky tonight."

Lana tossed her hair, sending the auburn ringlets she'd manufactured with a curling wand bouncing around her shoulders. "What makes you think you know better?"

"Oh my God." Courtney stared at her with wide eyes. "You're planning on getting laid. Who's the main target?"

"No one you know." It wasn't really a lie because Courtney

hadn't met Brody officially. Lana wasn't ready to share her plans with Courtney, lest the other woman laugh at her. Lana wouldn't blame Courtney if she did. In her more sensible moments even she had to admit getting Brody into bed tonight was probably a pipe dream.

The improbability of success didn't stop Lana from indulging the fantasy. However minor, there was a chance she could pique Brody's curiosity enough that he might push things a little further than he had the other night—a lot further, she hoped. She'd waited three years for a kiss, she wouldn't wait another three for the next one.

There *would* be a next one if she had anything to say about it.

Lana was saved from additional interrogation when the sound of a car engine punctured the afternoon quiet. The gathering turned as one and watched as an antique convertible car pulled to a stop and Sidney McCall hopped out. Leaving her bridesmaid to race after her, she lifted the flowing skirt of her strapless champagne satin dress and raced halfway up the aisle. "Hi, honey," she called out to Drew. "Sorry I'm late. Stupid car had a flat tire."

"It's okay," Drew replied, looking equal parts relieved and besotted. "I knew you were coming."

Brody cleared his throat pointedly and everyone laughed, the entire gathering having witnessed Drew's obvious anxiety over the bride's delayed arrival.

A young musician with long hair began playing an old Bryan Adams ballad on his guitar, and after some shuffling, Sidney allowed her bridesmaid to precede her toward the altar. Lana assessed the voluptuous brunette dressed in fitted, mint green silk. Dark glossy hair piled on her head so sexy ringlets tickled her nape, big brown eyes and even bigger boobs. Lana glanced down at the modest décolletage she'd needed underwire and padding to enhance, and felt her hopes dwindling. That woman was going to be dancing with Brody all night. Lana sent up a prayer that she was married or gay.

As the maid of honor took her place, she sent Brody a look filled with promise that anyone could have interpreted. Nope. Not gay. Darn it.

As if seducing Brody wasn't already a long shot, now Lana had to compete with the bridesmaid from hell.

Amy Walsh had a really nice set of tits. Brody couldn't understand why he wasn't more interested in them.

As the song ended and the band smoothly played into another one, Sidney's bridesmaid made no move to step away and Brody missed his chance to extricate himself politely. So he moved through another dance and made the occasional expected comment as she told him all about her ex-boyfriend, who was evidently a dropkick, and her cat, who apparently had fur balls.

Amy also had big, pretty brown eyes that were sending him all kinds of messages about her availability. But for some reason his gaze kept straying over her shoulder to scan the room. He had no idea what he was looking for until he found it.

Lana.

She was dancing with Mick Jensen. Brody remembered that she'd made excuses for the chef's early departure the other night and wondered if they had a thing going on. The guy said something to her and Lana laughed so hard she had to cling to his shoulders for support. Those long tapered fingers stood out, the nails newly painted a shiny lilac, against the dark fabric of Mick's shirt. Brody knew a yen to see those pretty fingers resting against *his* shirt, toying with the buttons until they popped open and slipping inside the material to touch flesh.

He'd been envisaging all manner of similar scenarios for three days and it didn't make a bit of sense. That heat that had risen between them had to have been a fluke. The kiss had surely been some peculiar impulse, one he definitely shouldn't have acted on. But tonight he was more interested in watching Lana dancing with somebody else than he was in flirting with the woman in his arms. It didn't seem normal.

"So what do you do for excitement around here?" Amy inquired, dragging his attention away from the other dancing couple. She eyed him through her thick lashes. "I guess in a small town you have to make your own fun."

"It's not so bad. I spent some time in Sydney when I was younger. The city's not my thing." Like it or not, Graceville was home. He'd realized it as he sailed back into Knight's Bay this time, when a sense of rightness had settled in his bones. Not all his memories of this town were good ones, but the place was part of him and the easy pace agreed with his sensibilities. He couldn't see himself living anywhere else.

"You sure? Because if you were ever up that way I'd be happy to show you the sights."

Brody chose to ignore the open invitation Amy's words presented. Why? She was just his type really. Available, uncomplicated and headed out of town tomorrow. He really couldn't figure why he had no interest in nailing her. She was pressed up against him in all the right places, but he remained consistently unstirred by the physical contact. The only female who'd gotten his juices flowing since Sidney was Lana.

To Amy, he said, "Thanks for the offer. I won't have time."

She blanched visibly at the brusque refusal and Brody felt a sweep of remorse that he'd offended her. But he had the feeling he wasn't going to change his mind about taking her home and he didn't want to spend the rest of the night fending her off.

The song ended and this time Amy seemed only too happy to put a bit of space between them. Fortunately, a few of the dancers started swapping partners, and Brody took the opportunity to hand Amy over to Drew's dad, Ray, which left Carol Buchanan without a partner.

She held her arms out to him and Brody got into position with ease. Drew's mother had taught him the fundamentals of waltzing way back when he'd been trying to impress some girl at high school. Trying to get into her pants more precisely, but he hadn't divulged that to Drew's mother at the time.

They chatted about the wedding but Brody's attention kept wandering to Lana and Mick. Was it his imagination or was she moving closer to the guy?

"She's a pretty girl."

Brody pulled his gaze back to his own dance partner. "Your son has good taste."

Carol laughed, her blue eyes crinkling at the corners. "I'm not talking about Sidney. I meant the girl you've had your eye on all night. Her name's Lana, isn't it? She works at the restaurant."

"I haven't had my eye on her." Complete bullshit, but Brody was surprised his preoccupation had been so obvious.

Carol gave him an admonishing look. "Brody Nash. You forget who you're talking to."

Brody felt the urge to squirm under the woman's sharp scrutiny. She'd always had had a talent for seeing everything, for knowing everything. All the secrets he'd never told about what it was really like living with his father. Why he'd swallowed his pride so many times and accepted Carol's open invitation to dinner with her family, even though it had made him feel like a stray dog she was too kind to shoo away.

"Why don't you just ask her to dance?"

Yeah right. Maybe he could lose his mind again and plant one on her, something she'd think was *fine*. Frankly, he was used to better reviews and the sting of her critique still hadn't quite dissipated. Perhaps that was why he was so preoccupied with her. "Nothing's going to happen there, so stop matchmaking."

"That would be quitting. Have you ever thought maybe it's time to stop sowing your wild oats and breaking hearts all along the eastern seaboard?"

Brody felt the beginnings of an honest-to-God blush creep up his neck. "Mrs. B, I promise I don't break hearts." He wasn't going to clarify one way or the other about his *wild oats*.

"Of course you do. Girls have been lining up for you for as long as I can remember."

"You've always been biased."

"If I am, I have good reason." Carol smiled up at him, a wealth of affection displayed on her elegant face. "You never realized how much I adored you, Brody—how much we all did. I used to wish one of my girls would take a shine to you but that never happened."

Brody laughed at the idea. "Belinda and Deanne did nothing but abuse me."

"Just like they did Drew. Abuse is the highest form of compliment from those two. Really, Brody, I don't think you've ever understood that we think of you as part of the family."

"You say it all the time. I get it."

"No, I don't think you do. Ray and I would have adopted you if we could have, if you'd just told the truth about what really went on in that house."

Brody turned away from her too-intelligent eyes. The urge to tell Carol to zip it was strong, but he could never speak that way to Drew's mother. Didn't she see talking about this shit always made him uneasy? He had no interest in delving into the past. It was long buried, along with his father, Larry. His mother hadn't taken an interest or bothered to give a good explanation for why she "couldn't handle being a mother", and had ultimately left going on twenty years ago. Francine Nash had never given a damn what had happened to him, so Brody figured he'd reciprocate. As far as he was concerned, when it came to his past there was nothing left to talk about.

Carol sighed. "I'm sorry I brought that up, sweetie. I've been feeling nostalgic today. Your youngest child tying the knot will do that to you. And I can't help but be very aware of the fact that none of this would be happening, that we wouldn't have Drew with us, if it weren't for you. You saved his life."

Brody didn't say anything. Speech was suddenly impossible over the massive lump in his throat. He hated it whenever Carol or Ray expressed any kind of appreciation for what he'd done all those years ago, when he'd been only twelve. He'd jumped into a flooding drain and yanked Drew's foot out of a grate that had hold of him. So what? Anyone who ever heard about the incident always seemed to look at him like he was some kind of hero, when the truth couldn't have been more different. Reckless instinct was part and parcel of who he was back then. He'd jumped into that water simply because that was the kind of crap he was willing to do. He'd taken a perverse satisfaction from dicing with his life. Altruism had nothing to do with it.

Applause smattered around the dance floor as the song came to an end. Carol didn't release him to add hers to the cacophony. Instead she leaned forward and kissed him on the cheek. She whispered in his ear, "I love you, sweetie. Try and accept it." Before she moved on to retrieve her husband from Amy, she threw over her shoulder, "And ask that girl to dance before someone else does."

Her comment made him seek Lana out with his gaze again, as he'd been doing all night—and being damned obvious about it apparently. Mick said something to her and walked off, leaving Lana without a dance partner. For a split second she appeared disorientated. That flash of little-girl-lost made Brody act on Carol's suggestion even though he'd had every intention of ignoring it.

He walked over and placed a hand on Lana's arm, stopping her as she looked set to leave the floor. She glanced at him, her eyes as wide and round as gold coins, her lips parted in surprise. He leaned in close in order to be heard over the opening bars of the next song and a light tangy fragrance tickled his nostrils. Her skin was softer than he'd expected, and the feel of her beneath his fingertips made them tingle in a way that shocked him, made his words gruff with demand. "Let's dance."

Lana felt herself gaping. She'd had only two glasses of champagne, but the room spun as though she were half-drunk. "You want to dance with me?"

Brody smiled thinly, as if her shock irritated him. "Yeah. Promise I won't bite."

His gaze passed over her in that thorough, assessing manner, resting for a moment too long on her throat. A hot chill swept through her, the thought of Brody and her throat and love bites preventing speech.

Taking a small step back, he released her arm, apparently

taking her silence as a refusal. "It was only an idea."

Comprehension finally caught up with her. Lana halted his egress with a hand on his arm. "No." She sounded panicked and breathless, and that wasn't the word she'd wanted to say at all. "I mean yes. Now. I want to. Dance with you, I mean." *Jeez, way to articulate, Lana.*

Something in his eyes flared, a mixture of heat and what she thought might be self-recrimination. Then he opened his arms and she moved into them like she was falling into heaven.

The band played Van Morrison and he smelled deliciously like subtle cologne and warm skin. With her in heels their faces aligned nicely. She would only have to tilt her head a little and their lips might brush. How would he react if she did it?

"Are you having a good time?"

Lana blinked and raised her eyes to his. "It was a lovely ceremony. They're such a great couple."

"I know."

Lana thought of his speech, which had been short but poignant. What he'd said about the bride had made every female in the room expel a collective sigh. *To Sid. If you could pick the perfect woman out of a catalogue, honey, you'd be it.*

Yes, blonde and vivacious was definitely Brody's thing. Still, it was a full moon tonight, and everyone liked to try something different every now and again. She was dancing with him, which was a start.

Her gaze roved over his clean-shaven jaw. "I saw Rufus didn't get called into service."

He grinned. "I managed to find a razor. I didn't want to spook anyone else."

"You weren't that scary. The beard was very..." she searched for a suitable descriptor, "...rakish. I like this look better though."

Lana's heart raced at her bold words, the flirtatiousness inherent in them. She averted her eyes, avoiding the sharp focus in his before she remembered she'd promised herself she wouldn't do that tonight. If Brody showed even the slightest interest she wanted to capitalize on it.

Resolutely, she turned back to face him. His attention was trained on her neckline, and Lana decided all the work she'd done to create cleavage had been worth the effort.

Catching her gaze, he said a little huskily, "Nice dress."

"Thanks. I bought it off the Internet." *Great, Lana. He really wanted to know that.* She flushed. "Sorry. Champagne makes me babble."

"No problem. Babble away."

Assuming he didn't mean it literally, Lana remained silent. She dared to move a little closer, wanting to sink further into the virile masculine heat he was giving off. He turned his head and their cheeks brushed. Lana held her breath, wondering if the move had been intentional. From the way his chest seemed to still against hers she didn't think so.

They danced like that for what seemed an eternity, encapsulated in a perfect little bubble. For once, Lana was glad she was tall for a female. Her steps easily matched his and her face fit perfectly into the curve of his neck. Without stopping to talk herself out of the impulsive gesture, she turned and brushed her lips lightly over his throat.

The hand resting on her hip flexed, anchoring harder to her flesh. "Christ, Lana," he rasped against her ear. "What the hell are you doing?"

"I don't know." She really didn't. She had no clue how this was happening, how he seemed to lean closer to her with each dance step, how she was managing to somehow draw him in with the sway of her body. "What do you think I'm doing?"

"Coming on to me."

"Is there anything wrong with that?"

"I'm not the kind of guy you should tease. I might take you seriously."

One could only hope. Lana's pulse thundered in her ears, so she was barely aware of when Van Morrison ended and Eric Clapton began. "Who says I'm not serious?"

"I do. You're not exactly…"

When his words trailed off Lana filled in, "I'm not your type."

His soft chuckle tickled her earlobe. "Lana, female's my type. I was going to say you're not the kind of girl who flirts with the likes of me. Perhaps you ought to ease up on the champagne."

"I'm not drunk. And I'm not a girl."

His hand moved from her hip, sliding around to the small of her back. He used the grip to draw her toward him until her breasts settled close to his chest. "I did notice that. But this— it's not a good idea."

"Do you ever do things just because you want to?"

"All the time. Too damned often. I don't always think before I act."

Lana sighed wistfully, thinking of all the years she'd done her best to be good, decent, unobtrusive. Of how it had gotten her nowhere while a few audacious moves had her right where she wanted to be. "I envy that."

"Most people would tell you it's not a virtue."

"Being virtuous isn't all it's cracked up to be," she said, using his retort of the other night.

"What is it you want, Lana?" he demanded, his voice suddenly terse. "You want me to find one of the empty rooms here, take you there and fuck you senseless? Because I'm warning you, I'm not above it."

The sound of applause penetrated the hazy cloud of thrilling desire that had woven around her. Lana felt stung, as if he'd slapped her. One part of her recognized that, as crude as the suggestion was, it wasn't without appeal. Perhaps she wasn't above it, either. Yet another, more sensitive part knew he wasn't really offering, but being intentionally rude in order to send her away. That he would go to that much trouble to put her off made her feel acutely unwanted.

She took a step back, leaving the heat of his embrace, feeling very much like she'd been burned. "Sorry, I forgot for a moment."

"Forgot what?" His voice sounded choked.

"That I'm dull and ordinary and not nearly daring enough to interest you." She couldn't believe she'd failed to remember that, even for a few short moments. "Thanks for the dance. Excuse me."

She managed to leave the floor without running like she wanted to. Lana decided to view that as a victory.

Chapter Three

Brody figured he was going to kick himself tomorrow, but he couldn't let Lana leave like that. Following her outside, he found her standing on the balcony. The elegant outline of her shoulders, the flowing lines of that silky dress silhouetted against the backdrop of the moon-gilded bay made her look like a mythical beauty, ethereal and unattainable.

But she wasn't unattainable. She'd made that pretty clear back on the dance floor before he'd fucked things up. Why had he done that anyway?

The rapid thump of his heart gave the answer as he crossed the balcony tiles. Something about her made him feel almost imperiled. He was intimidated by sweet, whip-thin Lana Green.

Crazy.

Lifting a hand, Brody touched it to her shoulder. She stiffened beneath his palm and he curled his fingers over her skin. "I'm sorry I said that in there. It was rude."

There was a pause before she spoke and when she did her voice was half-missing. "It's all right."

Brody's stomach dropped when he realized she'd been crying. "Jesus, Lana, don't cry. Not because of me." Regret seared him. "You're not dull or ordinary."

"You don't have to say that. I know I made a fool of myself."

She lifted a shoulder. "I just thought the forward approach might be worth a try."

She made to move away, but he circled her wrist with his fingers, feeling the way her pulse jumped beneath his touch. Her eyes widened when he drew her toward him. He felt the soft imprint of her breasts against his chest and it made him as hard as it had out on the dance floor. Harder now, because there wasn't such a critical need to mask his reaction.

Reaching up, he sank his hands into the softness of her hair, awakening that spicy apple scent. "It was worth a try," he said, and brought her mouth to his.

She sighed against him and immediately her lips parted. A relieved, hungry sound fell out of her and called to him, made his actions speed swiftly toward urgency. He settled her against the cool stucco of the wall and pressed into her. Concealed from the guests inside by a potted palm, Brody kissed her like there was no tomorrow, no good or bad choices. Making sure he did a more exhaustive job of it than he had last time, he nibbled at her lips, sucked gently on her tongue and barely held back from flat-out devouring her. He didn't stop until he ran out of air and she lay boneless against the wall.

The breath gasped into her in one long drag when he pulled away. She stared at him, her eyes wide with wonder, her lips plump and not as artfully painted as they had been. Her hair was mussed, a riotous cloud around her face. Moonlight did amazing things for her sex appeal.

"Wow," she said at last. "That was some kiss."

"Damn straight," Brody agreed. "Better than fine."

She laughed softly. "Oh. Was your pride hurt?"

"Doesn't take much."

Her gaze drifted over him with such blatant appreciation that he sucked in a breath. "No way should your ego be fragile."

Like a bullet train gone off the rails, there was no stopping him. Brody swept her up in his arms again and reveled in her instant response. She kissed like a wild creature who lived for nothing but this, as natural and committed to the process as a bird is to flight. When he lifted a hand between them and settled it over the slight swell of one breast she didn't flinch or hesitate. Arching into his touch, she breathed a word into his mouth that killed him, then brought him back to life.

Yes.

Releasing her mouth, Brody dropped his gaze to the place where he cupped her in his hand. The strap of her dress slipped down her arm, exposing the barest hint of pink lace. *Pink.* In his experience women usually wore black, as though it came as a package deal with the evening dress. But Lana wore pink and he was reminded once again that she was no ordinary woman. He really ought to tread carefully, because although he was by no means a monk, he also sensed that he'd never been anywhere quite like this with a woman before.

He brushed his fingers lightly over the edge of her strapless bra. There was barely anything to it. He watched, his hunger growing ferocious, as her flesh quivered, expanding so the lace tautened over the pebbling tip of her breast.

Suddenly the words *tread carefully* seemed like a foreign language. With little more than an encouraging tug, the lace dropped and Lana's ripe, dusky nipple popped out. "Sweet Jesus. I'm headed for trouble."

He took that enticing nub between his thumb and forefinger and gently pinched. Lana gasped and curled away from the wall, into his hand. "Take me with you."

"Excuse me, Mr. Nash?"

The chirpy pep of the wedding coordinator's voice had never grated on Brody's nerves as much as at that moment. He turned slightly to face the woman wearing a red power suit and a smile, shielding Lana from sight as he did so. "Yeah?"

"Mr. and Mrs. Buchanan are preparing to cut the cake. We need everyone to gather inside."

It took him a moment to realize the Mr. and Mrs. Buchanan she referred to were Drew and Sidney, not Drew's parents like he'd initially thought. One of these days he would have to get used to his best mate being a married man. "Right. We'll be in shortly."

The woman disappeared with a satisfied nod, the glass door swinging closed with a thud that once again muffled the music filtering out from inside. Laughter drifted up from somewhere below them, a couple out getting some fresh air. They weren't alone, yet he'd gone at Lana like they had been.

Well, almost. If they'd had complete privacy he wouldn't have stopped.

Turning back to her he saw that she'd covered herself, that pale, hard-tipped mound of soft flesh now hidden from view. Damn shame. "I didn't mean to go that far," he said. "But I can't say I'm sorry."

To his surprise when she met his eyes there was nothing but mischievous glee in hers. "Me neither."

As if he hadn't already been hard enough. "I wasn't serious inside when I said we could find an empty room. But it's not the kind of thing I'd stop at on moral grounds." He held her gaze. "Are you sure you want to get involved with a guy like that?"

Her lips curled slowly. "Yes."

He expelled a long sigh. "You should go inside."

She took a couple of steps toward the door then stopped, turning back to look at him. "Aren't you coming?"

Not yet, but I will be. "I need a minute."

It took her a moment to comprehend his meaning. When she did her eyes dipped to his crotch before immediately skittering away, as if she was ashamed of the fact she'd given him a hard-on he was having trouble getting rid of. Most women wouldn't be, but Lana wasn't most women.

Yet she was, most definitely, a woman, one who apparently wanted him. Brody was not prone to throwing away opportunities like this one.

He closed the distance between them and looked down into her face. "You know where I live?"

She laughed a little. "Yes."

"Once this thing is over you might want to stop by. I'll give you the grand tour."

She smiled, unconfused about what that meant. "I'd like that."

Although his cock still strained against his fly, an irritant with only one satisfactory cure, he said, "If you change your mind, Lana, no harm done."

A touch of irony tempered her smile. "I won't change my mind."

Brody watched her walk away, her strides assured and elegant. There were few things hotter than a woman who knew what she wanted. He was going to seriously enjoy giving Lana just that.

A few minutes later the cool night air had finally worked its magic. Brody had himself more or less under control when he turned to see Drew stepping out onto the balcony. "So this is where you've been hiding."

"Just enjoying the view." He thought of Lana's sweet little breast cupped in his palm and tried not to smile.

"As soon as we've finished the obligatory stuff, we're going to head off. Don't even think you're going to get out of saying goodbye."

"Wouldn't dream of it." Drew and Sidney planned to spend tonight at a nearby five-star hotel, bonking each other's brains out most likely, before flying out tomorrow for a fortnight in Mauritius.

"Was that Lana I saw you talking to out here?"

All of a sudden Drew didn't seem in such a big hurry to go back inside, and Brody took his lead, slowing his progress toward the door. "Yeah."

"She looks good, doesn't she?"

Brody tried for a nonchalant shrug. "Suppose. If you like the skinny type."

"She's not that skinny and you're not that fussy."

"Are you making a point here?"

He heaved a sigh. "Hey, don't tell Sidney this but Lana's the best waitress I've got. Knows how to do everything at that place. If she could cook, she could run it."

"Maybe you should have put her in charge."

"I thought about it." Drew grinned. "But I trust you."

A ribbon of warmth curled inside Brody, bringing humor along with it as a cloak. "Give us a kiss then."

"Shove it, Nash." Drew laughed and clapped him on the shoulder. "All I'm saying is, I'd hate for Lana to quit. Say, if something happened to upset her."

Brody recalled how he'd driven her to quiet tears not so long ago, the memory and its implication killing what was left of his libido. Disappointment ripped through him. How could he have forgotten he had responsibilities now? Two weeks of being a stand-up citizen, that was all Drew had asked of him. Surely he could at least try to do that.

He thought of Lana's wild kiss and the brave, arousing way she'd come on to him. His words sounded bitter. "I get your point."

"I figured you would."

It was nearly midnight by the time Lana climbed aboard the *Sunset.*

The bouquet had been tossed and through valiant effort Amy ensured she caught it. With smug satisfaction she took the flowers as well as Mick and his blue silk garter off the dance floor and neither of them were seen again. Courtney seemed inordinately irritated by the whole scenario, whether because she'd missed out on the flowers or Mick's hitherto constant attention, Lana wasn't sure. She drank far too much champagne and Lana avoided keeping pace with her, a decision she later congratulated herself for when she was as sober as a judge and Courtney had her head in the toilet.

"All I want is a nice guy. Just one nice guy," Courtney had wailed between bouts of retching. "Someone with a decent job and no Internet porn fetish. Is that too much to ask?"

Lana refrained from pointing out that Mick was actually a pretty nice guy once you got to know him and he had a decent job. But she couldn't swear either way on the Internet porn, so she kept her trap shut while she held back Courtney's long brown hair and patted her shoulder soothingly.

Shortly afterward, the crew from the Grill—*sans* Mick Jensen—called a maxi taxi and headed into town to continue the festivities at O'Ryan's Pub. Dropping a sore and sorry Courtney off on the way, Lana joined the others for a drink but spent most of the time staring out the window that fronted onto the street. It gave a good view of the marina, only a few hundred meters away. When she could extricate herself from the group without being noticed, she slipped out of the pub and walked the short distance.

Now she found herself on the deck of Brody's yacht, her shoes in hand. Fiddling with the latch that led to the lower cabin, she eventually got it open and slipped down into the warm darkness.

It took her eyes a moment to adjust. Then she managed to make out the dark paneling and navy blue upholstery. Moonlight streamed in a porthole, glancing off the stainless-steel galley and what she guessed was navigational equipment. In such a small space it wasn't difficult to locate the cabin Brody slept in.

The bed was neatly made, draped in a navy quilt. Indecision gripped Lana. Should she sit on the bed and wait? If so, would under or on top of the sheets be better? She was a virgin and had never been this close to a man's bed before. She had no idea what to do.

He invited you, Lana. Relax.

Smiling to herself, Lana climbed on top of the quilt and stretched out. Yes, Brody had invited her, had promised the *grand tour*. Very soon, she was going to have sex for the first time.

Inhaling, Lana let Brody's aura into her lungs, her body. The quilt smelled like him, a mixture of soap and salt. She recalled his touch on her breast earlier tonight, and her nipples beaded inside her bra, making her shift restlessly where she lay. Her panties, damp already from that balcony interlude, flooded with renewed arousal. Lord, when Brody got here she was going to combust the second he touched her.

When was he going to get here anyway?

Grappling with her evening purse, Lana found her mobile and checked the time. A few minutes past midnight. That wasn't so late. He probably felt he should wait around until Drew's parents left the wedding. Why, she didn't know but she wasn't going to get worked up about it. So he wasn't *rushing* here to be with her. He *had* invited her. Surely he wouldn't have forgotten.

Fear's icy fingers unfurled in her stomach. What if he'd changed his mind?

No, Lana. Don't be defeatist. Closing her eyes, she ran the memory of earlier tonight through her mind, like making a scene selection on her favorite DVD. She recalled the feel of his hands on her, his mouth possessing hers, so hungry it had seemed like he was starving for her. His body had been hot and strong as it pressed her against the wall. She'd felt something hard jutting against her and had suspected it was an erection. He'd later confirmed that.

She'd made him hard. He'd be here.

Her thoughts had longing mounting to uncontrollable proportions inside her. When she slipped her hand beneath the hem of her dress, the act was almost involuntary. The lace of her underwear was sodden where it rested against her swollen flesh. Pressing the heel of her hand to her mound relieved the building ache a little, not nearly enough. Lifting her hips, Lana slid the panties down her legs and off.

Her clitoris was so sensitive. When she touched a finger to it, it hummed like it was electrified. Lana moaned helplessly, circling the knot of flesh over and over again with her middle finger. How many times had she done this to herself while picturing Brody Nash with her mind's eye? How often had she uttered his name in a whisper as she took herself to the brink, wishing it was his hand moving on her? His fingers slipping inside her?

Inner walls clutching at the penetration, Lana fingered herself with practiced strokes while she thumbed her clit. Surrounded by Brody's masculine scent and the promise of what was soon to take place, climax came swiftly. Gasping his name as she had on so many previous occasions, she rode the waves to the shore, where she lay thrilled and spent on the sand. Ecstatically alive but as alone as a shipwrecked castaway.

But not for long, not this time. Keeping her eyes closed she felt herself drifting, sure that Brody would be here any minute.

Something made her wake with a start. Lana's heart pounded in her chest, her ears straining until she heard a metallic sound—the yacht's rigging rattling in a strong breeze that hadn't been evident before. Moonlight still bathed the cabin in pale light, but time had passed. How long had she been asleep?

Intent on finding her purse, Lana sat up. It was then she saw the shadowy figure sitting on the end of the bed. Instinct made her open her mouth to scream but a large, rough hand clamped over it.

"It's okay. It's me."

Fear dissipated but her heart rate remained erratic when Lana recognized Brody's voice. After a moment he dropped his hand. "I keep spooking you. I don't mean to."

"What time is it?"

"Almost two. I thought you'd be gone."

Lana's neck prickled, embarrassed heat rising through her. He'd deliberately waited, assuming she would give up and go home. "Oh my God. I'm so stupid. I thought you meant it, but— Oh God. I'll go." *I'll go away and die of humiliation.*

Planting a hand on the mattress either side of her, he stopped her from leaving. "I meant it."

With his face so close to hers, Lana smelled the rum on his breath. "Is that why you spent the last few hours drinking and waiting so late you thought I'd have left?"

"I was trying to do the right thing. You shouldn't have come."

Annoyance sparked to life. "You asked me to."

His touch was soft on her cheek as his eyes roamed over her face. "I know, but Drew reminded me we're supposed to be working together."

"So? I can handle going to bed with someone I work with."

He scowled. "Really?"

Lana realized she'd made it sound like a habit she'd acquired. Not wanting to follow that conversational path, she decided instead to concentrate on him. On the fact that he was here, that he hadn't moved away as a man who wanted her to leave might have.

The moonlight filtering in through the hatch in the ceiling of the cabin bathed him in cerulean light. He'd removed his bow tie and jacket, and the crisp white of his dress shirt took on a fluorescent appearance. Lana's gaze drifted downward to examine the V of skin revealed by the two buttons he'd undone, and her mouth dried out. Lana reached out and toyed with the shirt. She felt the heat of his flesh through the soft fabric and knew hers must be as hot to the touch.

His breath caught sharply when she released the next button, his shock mirrored by the way her heart slammed against her ribs. Even as the audacity of her own actions stunned her, Lana slid her fingers down and worked on the next button until it too was free of its hole.

Her question was barely audible. "Do you want me to leave?"

She was terrified he'd say yes, but he said nothing at all as she slowly, methodically released every last fastening. When she was done the material hung open to reveal a strip of his chest—toned flesh covered in fine dark hair. She'd never seen him with his shirt off before, and he looked better than she'd ever imagined.

Reaching out, she touched her fingers to all that hard packed muscle. He was so strong, so solid. Touching him alone made the wetness between her thighs increase, made her true feelings slip out. "Wow. You're so sexy."

"Hell, Lana." His voice was raspy, making Lana aware her actions had impacted him. "You make it impossible for a man to kick you out of bed."

"Are you trying to?"

"Yes." He encircled her wrist with his fingers, stilling the wandering exploration of her hand. Glancing up, she met his gaze. His dark chocolate eyes shone in the dim light, their depths reflecting the battle going on inside him. Tense lines bracketed his mouth, and his heart beat a rapid tattoo against her palm. "You should get out of here while you still have the chance."

Lana shook her head, never tearing her eyes from his. "I've used up all my chances tonight. If you want me to leave, you might have to carry me out."

He snaked an arm around her back and grasped her thigh with his other hand. For a moment Lana was sure he was going to do exactly as she'd suggested. Mortification ripped through her. That would be a great look, being hauled down the wharf and unceremoniously dumped in the parking lot.

Perhaps it was his intention to get rid of her, but the instant he pulled her forward and their chests meshed together, he stilled. The action had brought their faces close, and Lana watched as the fight in his eyes turned to surrender. His grip on her thigh tightened and he drew her leg snugly around his hip. Then he made a guttural sound and leaned forward to capture her lips with his.

He devoured her mouth like a man starved. Lana tried to keep up, to give as good as she got, but the sensuous thrust of his tongue, the tantalizing scrape of his teeth overwhelmed her so all she was capable of was a primal response. Where he led, she followed. When he touched—her face, her hair, her breasts—she offered herself outright. What he demanded, she let him take.

His movements were hurried as he pulled her arms out of the straps of her dress. "Do you have any idea how much I've wanted to do this all night?" His move had exposed her bra, and he brushed his fingers over the lace. "Pink. You're such a cute little surprise package."

With a deft flick of his fingers her bra disappeared. Instinctively, Lana crossed her arms over her chest. She'd tried not to think about the part of this plan of hers that involved Brody seeing her naked. "It was padded." From the astounded look on his face, she deduced he was wondering how her cleavage could have been so misleading. "I can eat whatever I want and I never seem to put on weight. Other women hate me for it but I always wished I had more…" She glanced down at herself. "Well, more of everything."

Something in his eyes softened, and his smile reassured her. His touch became gentle as he uncrossed her arms and set them away from her body. Lana tried not to squirm as he looked at her. "You're gorgeous," he uttered.

Lana released a nervous laugh, which died in her throat when Brody dipped his head and nuzzled her breasts. His breath was hot on her flesh, the slight rasp of his chin an erotic sensation. When he took her nipple into his mouth and rolled his tongue over it, she cried out at the shock of exquisiteness. All the times she'd imagined what this would be like hadn't prepared her for the wonderful whirlpool of pleasure that spun inside her. "Oh, I can't believe how good that feels."

"You're unbelievable. Taste like honey. God, Lana." She fell back on the bed as he moved over her, his touch growing more urgent as it skimmed down her side and tugged off her dress. He slid his hand over her hip and into the valley between her thighs. When he encountered her exposed folds, a groan spilled out of him and his teeth grazed her throat. "No panties. *Jesus.*"

Lana's hips jolted from the mattress when he ran his finger over her clit. She clutched his shoulders and whimpered, tugging at his dress shirt. "Off. Take this off."

With jerky movements, Brody stripped away the shirt and discarded it, falling on her once again to feast on her breasts.

Sensation burned inside her, heat mounting, spiraling from the inside out. His mouth on her flesh was incredible, the untamed desperation of his kisses exhilarating. Her hands moved to his waistband, a blatant urging that he had no trouble interpreting. He yanked down his zipper and pushed his pants down his legs.

He reached above her head to open a hideaway cabinet and rifle through it. Lana took the opportunity to satisfy her curiosity, slipping her hands down his hair-roughened chest and flat stomach until she came up against something rigid and hot. And *big*. She curled her fingers around it and her heart thundered. He was larger, thicker and more unyielding than she'd ever expected.

"You okay?"

Returning her gaze to his face she saw a sardonic smile curving his lips. Was he beginning to realize how inexperienced she was? She schooled herself to smile, hoping she would appear worldly and eager, instead of daunted by his potential to hurt her. "Never been better."

He moved his hips a little, the action causing his hard length to tunnel through her cupped hand. His skin was so smooth and sleek, the strain of his flesh so strongly masculine that Lana's feminine muscles quivered in anticipation, anxiety fleeing for the moment. Experimentally, she ran her fingers up and down his shaft, fascinated by the slight protrusion of veins running along the front of it. The tip of his penis was smooth and round, dampened by a drop of shiny, translucent liquid. Collecting some with her index finger, Lana brought it to her mouth and tasted him.

"*Fuck.* Lana, Christ, I need to..." He ran his hand up her thigh and dipped a finger into her moist center. "Tell me you can come while I'm inside you, because I don't want to wait."

Lana had no idea, but she doubted it, under the circumstances. She supposed now might be a good time to enlighten Brody of that particular situation, but somehow she knew he wouldn't be happy to hear he was breaking new territory. It was close to dark, he was half-drunk. If she could keep it together he might never know. Lana would much prefer he never knew. "Maybe. Let's try."

She watched in fascination as he rose to his knees and rolled on the condom he'd retrieved, the sheen of latex making his cock seem bigger somehow. Her heart jumped nervously, but she told herself to calm down. Women did this all the time. She was so wet he'd probably slide in easily anyway. She hoped.

He lowered his body, aligning it above hers. His heat was overwhelming. The slow, purposeful way he parted her thighs and settled his pelvis between them made her hold her breath in mounting anticipation. He probed her wet entrance. She felt the shift in her muscles and it wasn't an unpleasant sensation. Lana moaned in pleasure and relief. This was going to be fine. Not going to hurt at all.

Her breath hitched when he pushed a little farther into her, spreading her flesh apart. "God, Lana, you're tight."

His comment made panic jolt inside her. Need he point it out? It felt as though he could barely fit into her, like her body was resisting him. Why, when she wanted him so much? Would he stop if he figured out the extent of her inexperience?

She couldn't let that happen. Grasping his hips, she clung to him, keeping him inside. "Now," she said. Perhaps it would be better to get this part over with quickly, like ripping off a band-aid. "I want you now."

Heat radiated from the spot where their bodies fused. He advanced again and her muscles clenched as though in protest. Pain sparked inside her and Lana was shocked at its intensity. God, how much farther did he have to go?

Framing her face with his hands Brody stared down at her. Astonishment and suspicion gathered in his expression. "Lana, tell me you're not a—"

"Don't stop," she interrupted him. Digging her fingernails into his lower back she arched her hips, inviting more of his thick rod into her. "Do it, please." She wanted him, had always wanted him to be her first. She had to see this through. Tilting her hips higher she wrapped her legs around his and felt the action propel him forward. He entered her completely with a throaty groan.

Lana bit her lip to stifle the exclamation that tried to burst from her mouth as her flesh gave way with an explosion of sensations. Sharp pain followed by a hot, thrumming ache. The way he stretched her was so alien that her breath came in rapid pants as she struggled to adjust to the incursion of his body into hers.

"Lana." Her name sounded low and dangerous on his tongue. She resisted the urge to hide from the accusation in his gaze, wanting to be strong in that at least, if she couldn't do this without giving away the shock and hurt of it. "Why the hell didn't you tell me this was your first time?"

Ignoring the question, she said again, "Don't stop. I want more."

The lines of his face turned implacable. Lana felt the imminence of his retreat and tightened her hold on him, digging her fingernails into the taut muscles of his backside and arching beneath him so he went deeper. He squeezed his eyes shut before burying his face against her collarbone, a tremor rippling through his chest. She shifted her pelvis against his. "This feels good, doesn't it?"

"For me," he said roughly, his voice muffled against her throat. "Not for you."

"It's getting better."

Brody propped his weight on his elbows and looked down at her, stern remonstrance marking his features. "You shouldn't have done this. Not with me."

She'd never had a choice about that—he was the only one she'd ever wanted. "It's done already." Lana touched the uncompromising lines of his face, memorizing the feel of his cheek beneath her hand because she sensed she might never get to touch him like this again. "I want to finish it."

Chapter Four

Brody figured Lana was going to get her wish a lot sooner than either of them would like. The taut heaven of her body gripping him felt so good, he teetered on a knife edge between the need to save her from further pain and the primitive urge to push himself harder, faster, rougher into her until he exploded.

Neither choice was acceptable. He was hurting her, and he couldn't stand the thought of that. But pulling out was impossible when she gripped him so firmly with everything she had—her twining limbs, her clamping heat, those determined eyes. She shifted her pelvis again and he groaned as the action made his cock hum with pleasure. Her stiff nipples brushed his chest as she writhed beneath him, notching the sensations higher. He'd never lost control like this with a woman but it was as though he was the one trapped beneath her, unable to evade the pleasure she tortured him with.

Fury mingled with the tugging physical needs and it took every ounce of will he possessed to retreat and reenter gently. Her breath hitched at the action and Brody gritted his teeth. Why hadn't she told him? If he'd known the extent of her innocence, there was no way he would have invited her here. He felt deceived, almost taken advantage of, which was ridiculous because he'd started this. He'd danced with her, kissed her, when he should have stayed far, far away.

He shifted inside her in short thrusts. "Does that hurt?"

She shook her head. "Feels better. Oh..." She trailed off on a sigh when he rotated his hips slowly. "That's nice."

Shit. Her sweet voice coming out on the back of quick little pants of exertion was playing havoc with his thinly held command. One full plunge into her snug body and it would be over. The press of her fingernails into his ass wasn't helping, but he liked the sharp bite too much to tell her to let him go. Sensation sparked on his nerve endings, frying his brain and muddling it even worse than the alcohol he'd consumed. He needed so badly to lose himself in her. The climax was rushing at him even as he tried to stave it off.

Forcing his movements to still, he held her gaze. "You're not going to be able to come like this."

"It doesn't matter."

She smiled softly as though she meant it. Brody meant what he said too. "Like hell it doesn't."

Slipping his hand between their bodies, he found the raised nub of her clit and rotated a finger over it. Her thighs quivered and clenched him tighter, pulling him farther into the hot fist of her feminine flesh. "Stop doing that," he demanded. "I'm having enough trouble here."

She merely continued to smile at his distress. "I want to make you come."

Christ. He kept stroking her clit, eliciting little mewling sounds that drove him insane. She wriggled her hips and arched high, accepting him to the hilt in her unused flesh. She moaned, her grip on his ass strengthening, pushing him harder, deeper inside her. "Brody...kiss me. Kiss me."

He did what she wanted and the feel of her lips moving with eager passion beneath his did him in. A kiss shouldn't have made him lose it completely but Lana's was pure, sweet magic.

He groaned into her mouth, his tongue dancing with hers as the tension gripped his lower body, the burning heat shooting through him until the reins slipped out of his hands. With one final thrust the fire spilled out of him and into her.

Dropping his head, he burrowed it into the fanning silk of her hair. It still smelled good, like it had when he'd first asked her to dance. It seemed that moment and this one were inextricably connected, as though the second he'd drawn her into his arms it was inevitable they'd end up here. As though he'd had no say in that, just as he'd had no mastery over what had just happened.

"Oh boy. That was...amazing. Truly, utterly amazing."

That was one way to put it. She was probably too polite to say *pretty fucking pathetic.* The lethargic contentment weighting his limbs mocked Brody. Here he was, sated and limp on top of her, and she hadn't even climaxed. He'd taken her virginity and given nothing in return. He felt like a thief.

Furious at himself as well as her for putting him in this untenable position, Brody pulled out of her as carefully as he could. He pushed up on his hands and studied her face, hard. "What the hell were you thinking?"

Her eyes went round at his tone. "I don't know what you mean."

"I mean you should have told me you were a virgin."

"Oh. That." She rolled to her side, presenting him with the curve of her shoulder. "I suppose."

"You suppose? Jesus, Lana. You can't spring something like that on a guy."

"I'm sorry if you were surprised."

This was probably one of those times when a more tender approach was called for, but tender had never been his forte.

"How old are you?"

"God, Brody, I'm not jailbait." She laughed bitterly and scooted to the end of the bed, where she curled her arms around her knees. "I'm twenty-three."

"Twenty-three," he repeated. "And you've never had a boyfriend?"

She shot him a look over her shoulder. "I don't have to give you all the details of my past. Unless you want to tell me about yours."

With a grunt of annoyance he moved to the edge of the bed, swinging his legs over the side. He reached for his trousers and started pulling them on. Beside him, he sensed Lana's discomfort and found her dress, handing it over without looking at her. For the life of him, he couldn't understand why she had done what she had with *him*. "This was a mistake."

She flinched at the cold certainty of his statement. "If it was, it was mine to make."

"Weren't you...saving it?"

She yanked on her dress with jerky movements. "For what—a rainy day?"

No, for someone special. Someone other than him. "You should have said something."

"I didn't think you'd want to know."

The implication being she didn't think he'd care. If she thought he was such an unfeeling bastard, why had she wanted to lose her virginity to him?

"Look, I know you don't have relationships, in case you think I've gotten the wrong idea." Derision made her voice hard. She didn't sound at all like the sweet thing who'd blushed while they were dancing and had responded to his kisses with such heat and joyfulness. "I wanted to have sex without worrying about getting into a relationship. I'm not looking for anything serious. Why would the fact I've never been with a man before change that?"

"Because you obviously have no idea what casual sex is."

"So you think virginity is synonymous with ignorance?" she asked. "I wanted to know what sex was like and I knew you were the kind of man who would give me that. Get the job done without all the hassle. That's all this was. You don't have to look so deathly afraid it might have actually meant something to me." She stood and strode out of the cabin.

Brody sat where he was, flummoxed by her admissions and her implied assessment of him. There was nothing in what she said he would refute. He didn't do relationships. He was fairly practiced at no-strings sex. So why did it feel like she'd cut him to the quick with her opinions? For some reason he hated the idea that Lana had thought of him as nothing more than a man who would *get the job done*. A convenient cock when she needed one.

Brody walked into the main saloon to find her already heading up the companionway. He stopped her with a hand on her arm. "I'll take you home."

"I can take care of myself. Besides, you shouldn't be driving."

He'd love to blame his abysmal performance entirely on alcohol but he wasn't as drunk as she seemed to think. Unfortunately. He should have stayed longer at O'Ryan's, reminiscing with his old boss. Maybe then he would have been too trashed to get it up. Instead he found himself unable to drive, yet capable enough to defile a virgin. Great. As if he didn't already know sleeping with her was the wrong thing to do, he had to live with that on his conscience.

Making a grab for his mobile, he punched in a number.

After a brief conversation he disconnected. "A friend of mine owns a taxi. Dave will come and get you. I'll walk you out."

"That's not necessary."

"Right. Because you're such a woman of the world."

She huffed in irritation and pulled herself up the companionway. Brody shrugged back into his dress shirt without bothering to button it and followed her.

Crossing her arms, Lana stared straight ahead as she marched up the dock. Her throat felt choked with cotton wool. She figured that might be the tears waiting to well out of her, but for now, thank God, she was too angry to release them.

How dare Brody act as though she should check with him first before she made decisions about her own body? How would he like it if she passed judgment on him? She wasn't ignorant of his habits. She'd seen him a few times over the years flirting with women at O'Ryan's Pub, leaving with them. Once, she'd been stopped at the traffic light in Main Street, not far from the marina, and she'd seen him walking a pretty blonde to her car. She remembered staring, her mouth agape, as the two of them kissed.

The fact they'd spent the night together had been unmistakable. She'd been in the first mad throes of her infatuation and she'd thought she'd give anything to be the one leaving his boat in the morning after a night of wild passion.

All things considered, the reality was a huge letdown.

They reached the marina car park, but the cab hadn't arrived. Brody seemed intent on waiting with her, and Lana didn't know how long she could keep up the coolly affronted act. "You can go."

"I'll wait." His tone brooked no argument. It gentled a little when he inquired, "Are you going to be okay?"

Now he asked her that. Ten minutes ago she wouldn't have minded being held a little while, being treated as special instead of contagious. It was too late for him to make a feeble attempt at chivalry now. "I'm not going to start stalking you. If you receive a dozen headless roses in the mail, don't look at me."

Annoyance tightened his voice. "I meant physically."

Stupid that after what she'd done with him discussing the condition of her anatomy should embarrass her. "You don't have to feel responsible for me, Brody. I know that's the last thing you'd want."

"What's that supposed to mean?"

"It means you're terrified enough of running the restaurant. You don't need to worry that deflowering virgins comes along with similar obligations."

"I'm not *terrified.* I'll do what has to be done because Drew trusts me."

"So do I." It made no logical sense, but her faith in him had always been an intrinsic thing. "You're good at what you do."

"Yeah well," he muttered. "Drew trusted me not to upset you and look what happened."

"Why would Drew be worried about me?"

"Because he doesn't want to lose you. Says he couldn't run the place without you."

"Really?" Drew had often said as much, but she'd thought his praise nothing more than a product of the easy charm he exuded. "He said that?"

His lips tilted. "Apparently you're good at what you do too."

She'd always secretly thought so, but it was exceedingly nice to know her efforts hadn't gone unnoticed. "I promise I won't quit on your watch, Brody. I have no desire to make you look bad."

His laugh was derisive. "Why in hell not?"

"Drew doesn't need to know anything about tonight," she reiterated. "It's between you and me."

Light passed over his face. The taxi's headlights, growing larger as the vehicle approached. After a moment he muttered softly, "You're an amazing person, Lana. I don't get why you came here tonight. If all you wanted was sex, you could have gotten it a long time ago. You must have had lots of interest."

Lana laughed. "Yeah right." When she realized he was dead serious, her heart curled with pleasure. Resolutely she tamped down the reaction. Her internal organs had no business reacting because Brody Nash had thrown her a compliment. It hardly made up for the insults of earlier. "Tell me something, Brody. If I hadn't been a virgin, if I'd been jumping into bed with the entire front row of the local football team, would you have asked me why I'd done that?"

"Of course not."

"Because it would have been none of your business, right?"

The cab came to a stop and the driver called out a greeting. Brody responded with a few words and Lana used the moment to settle into the back seat. She heard Brody tell Dave the driver to "take special care of her", and couldn't help but wish he'd done that himself.

No matter, she sighed. She'd gotten what she went looking for, her first experience with sex. So it hadn't been quite as romantic as she'd hoped—that was her fault for having those fanciful dreams in the first place. On some private level, she must have been harboring the fantasy that one night together and Brody would realize he had feelings for her.

Idiot.

The cab pulled away and Lana fought the urge to look back. In the end she couldn't resist and she turned in her seat, gazing out the back windscreen.

Brody was still standing there, watching, his dark figure growing smaller as the distance between them lengthened. Despite the obvious need to curtail her emotions where he was concerned, the sight of him clutched at her heart.

He looked so alone.

Chapter Five

"Are you on again tonight?"

"Yep, back at six," Lana said in answer to Courtney's question. Silverware spilled gleaming from the polishing cloth she held in her hand, clattering into the hutch. Closing the drawer with her hip, Lana glanced at her watch. "Three hours. I think I'll go home in the meantime." Split shifts were a fact of life when you worked in a restaurant, but Drew usually organized the rosters so they were kept to a minimum.

"Come shopping with me," Courtney suggested. "I have to get a new pair of shoes before these fall apart. We could grab a late lunch in town."

Lana grimaced. "My feet are killing me today. I don't think I want to deal with the extra walking around." She sent the other woman a sideways glance. "You could always ask Mick."

"To come shoe shopping? Every man's fantasy I'm sure."

It had become pretty clear to Lana that behind the chef's jovially suggestive comments was a fairly serious attraction to one Courtney Fitzsimmons. When she'd pressed him about the night of the wedding, he'd admitted that nothing happened between him and Amy, that he'd only flirted with her to make Courtney jealous.

For days now, she'd done her level best not to think about how Drew and Sidney's wedding night had ended for her. Mick and Courtney's shenanigans provided a convenient distraction.

She told Courtney, "He'd be happy to go with *you*."

"No he wouldn't."

"He likes you."

"Right. That's why he was all over that bridesmaid the other night. Why he went home with her."

"Courtney, you did nothing but abuse him at the wedding."

"So? If he really likes me why did he give up so quickly?"

Lana shook her head at Courtney's reasoning. It would never occur to Lana to test a man's feelings like that, not if she really cared about the outcome. Not that she'd ever been in a position to try. "Nothing happened between him and Amy. He told me so."

"Right, and men *always* tell the truth." Courtney sighed in frustration. "I don't want to talk about me. Let's talk about you for a change. Atmosphere's been a little chilly around here. I keep getting the feeling I'm missing something."

"You're not missing anything."

"Uh-huh." Courtney waited a heartbeat. "You like him, don't you?"

"Who, Mick? I told you we're just friends."

Courtney rolled her eyes. "I'm talking about Brody. It's obvious."

Lana hoped that wasn't true. "I've barely spoken to him."

"Exactly. You're friendly with all the guys except him. There's something fishy going on, I just know it."

"Lana."

They both turned with a guilty start at the sound of Brody's voice. There was nothing in his expression to indicate he'd overheard their conversation, but Lana's heart tripped all over itself anyway. She held his gaze for only a fleeting second before returning her attention to the cutlery in her hand. "Yes?"

"I need your help."

Surprised, she turned back to face him. She didn't think Brody had ever asked for her help before. "Really?"

"Drew's little instruction book says you're the best person to ask about computer problems around here, and I think I just stuffed something up."

Behind the expressionless mask she saw frustration and a touch of helplessness haunting his eyes. It was the helplessness that made it utterly impossible for her to say no. "I'll take a look."

Courtney's lips tilted as she took her leave and Lana followed Brody to the small office located at the back of the restaurant.

All the waterfront space was utilized for the restaurant's diners, so the office was a cramped windowless area that opened off the kitchen. The second Brody followed her into the room, Lana wished she had taken the bitchy route and refused to help him. The square footage couldn't have been a lot larger than an average jail cell.

Or the sleeping berth of a yacht.

Lana took a seat in the swivel chair behind the desk and tried valiantly to ignore the way Brody's big body took up so much of the space. The air conditioner was quietly emitting cool air into the room, but it did nothing to stop Lana from feeling flushed and intensely bothered by Brody's masculine aura. It enveloped her as he placed one hand on the desk beside her and one on the back of her chair so he could lean forward and look at the screen with her. She did her best to concentrate on the computer and not Brody's closeness.

"I was working on Drew's stock-management program and

the files I had open just disappeared."

"Computers aren't always predictable. Have you been using the Net?"

"A bit."

"Hmm. It's possible you've picked up a virus."

"Sounds nasty," he said drolly.

She turned her head before she could caution herself against it, meeting his gaze. His dark eyes were right there, as if he'd already been studying her profile. Lana's heart rushed forth and did somersaults an Olympic gymnast would envy. He was so close she could see the fine outbreak of stubble on his chin, feel the light brush of his breath feathering her temple.

"They can be." She cleared her throat. "All it takes is one click on the wrong link and you've got a gremlin in the works. Have you visited any suspicious sites recently?"

He arched a brow. "Are you asking if I've been trawling the web for porn?"

Well, she shouldn't have started this line of questioning. Even the joking reference to pornography had Lana thinking distinctly sexual thoughts, a dangerous proposition with him hovering over her shoulder. "Just checking." With an effort, Lana feigned indifference as she turned back to the computer. "I hear Horny Housewives dot com gets a lot of traffic." *Yep, I know all about Internet porn. Not so innocent after all, am I?*

"I'll keep that in mind," he drawled. "So if it's a virus, what does that mean?"

"I'll need to run a scan and try to restore the corrupted files. Then I could update your antivirus software and upgrade your firewall, just to be safe."

"Why didn't I think of that?" Brody quipped. She felt the heat of his stare once again resting on her profile. "So I guess you're pretty smart."

Lana felt herself flush with pleasure. "You don't have to be a super brain to understand computers. All it takes is practice."

"I saw the website you built for Drew. You did a good job. Makes me wonder why you're still hanging around Graceville when you could be working in the city for some big company."

"I don't want to live in the city, I like it here. Between the websites and the hours Drew gives me, I have plenty to do. Besides, I always thought maybe I'd open my own business one day."

"Yeah? What kind?"

His curiosity didn't seem contrived, but suddenly Lana felt silly for bringing up the subject. She shrugged uncomfortably. "I thought an Internet café would work well on Main Street. We're getting more backpackers coming through town all the time, and they all need to email home."

She turned to find him studying her again. "That's a really great idea."

"You think?"

"I wouldn't blow smoke up your skirt."

He smiled and Lana giggled at the silly saying. "That's a relief."

His gaze roamed, coming to rest on her mouth. When he lifted his eyes to hers, she read the desire swirling in their depths. Lana was helpless to stop the longing from building inside her.

Abruptly, he straightened, tearing his attention away from her. He gave his T-shirt a tug and walked around to the opposite side of the desk. "Sorry. I probably stink."

"You're fine." He'd opened up a world of sensation the other night, then given little more than a taste before retreating as though she'd had no right of entry in the first place. It wasn't fair. She forcibly returned her attention to the computer screen. "I'll have a fiddle around here and see if I can retrieve your documents. There's no guarantee your work will be saved though."

"Whatever you can do is great. How long do you think it'll take?"

"Depends. An hour or so maybe."

He winced. "This is your break isn't it? I'll make sure you get paid."

"Can you afford the going rate for a computer technician?"

Lips tilting at her sassy remark, he said, "I'll have to ask Drew."

Her heart gave a wild kick in response to his smile. He was so devastatingly handsome when he dropped that glowering countenance that kept people at bay. It was like staring into a dark, forbidding lake and discovering the silt bottom concealed a bounty in precious jewels. It made Lana want to dive right in and submerse herself.

He's a big, insensitive ass, she reminded herself firmly. *Treated your virginity like leprosy. Doesn't care about you.*

"The sooner I get started the better." The need to self-defend made her words sound harsh, as though she was trying to get rid of him. A necessity in the circumstances. Lana felt cornered in the room, which suddenly seemed practically airless.

"Right. I'll be here in the kitchen if you need anything."

When he was gone, Lana let out the breath that had been locked in her lungs. Resolutely, she focused her attention on the computer and got to work.

Ten minutes later, while she was waiting for the new

antivirus software to download, Lana found her gaze wandering idly over the various accoutrements littering the desk—the disheveled looking in-box, the photo of Drew and Sidney stuck to the side of the computer monitor. Beneath a manila folder marked *receipts*, she saw the corner of a book poking out. Lifting the folder, she read the cover. *Heart of Darkness* by Joseph Conrad. Lana remembered having been forced to read it in school, and struggling to wade through an analysis of the imagery of darkness and isolation. Brody read something like that for leisure and he called *her* smart?

"Are you hungry?"

Lana started, glancing up to see Brody once again filling the doorway. He gripped the doorframe above his head with both hands, the stance emphasizing his height and the breadth of his chest where his plain black T-shirt stretched over it. The hem rode up, exposing a strip of flat stomach above the waistband of his checkered chef's trousers. Lana found herself staring in fascination at the slight indent of his navel, wondering what it would be like to run her tongue around its circumference and all the way up his chest to his mouth. Or down to his...

"Lana? You haven't had lunch have you?"

She snapped her attention to his face. His mouth was curved in what she could only define as a satisfied smirk, and she knew without a doubt he'd read her mind. She also had the distinct feeling he'd been trying to educe lustful thoughts in her. Why? So he could prove to himself he could have her if he chose—even though he didn't want her?

"I haven't eaten," she said, seething with frustration of more types than one.

"I'll cook you something. I have a great piece of salmon I could grill. Or I was about to try out an idea for a new dessert, if you want to be my taster."

For dessert, Lana. He wants you to taste his dessert. "What kind are we talking about?"

"You like chocolate?"

"Is that thing about the Pope being Catholic still true?"

He smiled, the smugness notching up considerably, and dropped his arms from the doorframe. "I'll be back shortly."

It must have taken Lana a good ten minutes to reestablish the concentration required to make progress on her PC fix-it job. She heard him out there in the kitchen, moving around, listening to an FM radio station that played new alternative music alongside rock-and-roll classics.

A man who looked like he did shouldn't also have an interest in classic literature and the talent for creating wicked chocolate delights. It turned him from your run-of-the-mill sexy guy to a walking, talking fantasy man. Her fantasy man, still, no matter how staunchly she tried to remember that he could just as easily be a supercilious jerk five minutes after he'd melted her with seductive words and a hot stare.

Was she ever going to shake her infatuation with him?

Forty minutes later, Brody placed a warm choc-cheese cupcake on a plate, added a side of brandy-soaked strawberries and took it into the office.

Lana glanced up from the computer monitor. The cute little furrow in her brow smoothed out as she eyed the plate, a ravenous sparkle lighting her eyes. It reminded Brody of the way she'd looked at him the other night when he'd gotten naked, and the way she'd undressed him with her eyes a little while ago. His blood stirred hot in his veins, making a mockery of his recent attempts to follow her example and act like nothing had happened between them.

"How are you doing in here?"

"Almost done."

He handed her the plate and she tucked into the dessert with apparent relish, uttering little mewling noises of delight that made him remember a pink lace bra, *no panties,* and smooth, slender legs wrapped tight around him. Because his boxer briefs started to feel too snug, he took a seat in the vinyl chair opposite the desk and crossed one foot over the opposite knee.

He'd never realized before how integral Lana was to this place, but now he knew what Drew had been talking about. Floor service worked like a well-oiled machine when she was here, but the gears became sticky when she wasn't. She'd only had one day off in the five since the wedding, but her absence had been noticed.

Not only from a work perspective, God help him. He wanted her again, hadn't been able to think of his appalling performance the other night without kicking himself. There she'd been, a gorgeous woman new at the whole sex arena, and instead of guiding her gently into it, he'd fallen on her clumsily the minute he'd found her lying in his bed. With half a gut full of rum and months' worth of deprivation fuelling his actions, he'd only been out for what he could get, not for what he could give her.

Not his proudest moment. No wonder her attitude toward him had cooled.

"Oh God," she exclaimed, her eyes rolling back in her head when she got halfway through his creation. She pointed her spoon at the plate. "It's a little chocolate cake with cheesecake in the middle."

Brody felt ridiculously pleased, a bit like the Einstein of

chocolate cupcakes. The high praise bolstered his flagging ego. Maybe she would put *great cook* on his pro list, right opposite *bad lover* on the con side. "You like it."

"It's divine."

"I was thinking I'd serve it with a chocolate ganache and some fresh strawberries." She tilted her head a little doubtfully, prompting him to ask, "What do you think?"

"Honestly? The ganache might be overkill. Yes to the strawberries and a little King Island cream, but that's it." She glanced up and gave him a bashfully playful grin. "It's just my opinion, but chocolate sauce would make this too much sin for one sitting."

He sent her a knowing smile. "Lana, there's no such thing."

She ducked her head and concentrated on picking up crumbs of cupcake with a long finger and popping them into her mouth. "If you say so."

Watching that finger slide in between her lips had banked lust escaping. Once again he was acutely aware of the fact he hadn't given her an orgasm the other night. Never had he been in a position where it was so glaringly obvious a woman got more satisfaction from chocolate than from him.

"Are you a forgiving person, Lana?" He realized as he asked that he already knew the answer. The fact that she'd gone out of her way to help him today, without making him feel like a chump for being less than tech savvy, told its own story.

She looked at him square on. "I suppose so."

"I acted like a prize jerk the other night. You didn't deserve that and you were right—your past is none of my business. Think you can forgive me?"

Her lips curved into a smile that was as warm and sweet as simmering honey. "Yes."

Damn she was pretty. That smile shot straight to his crotch, grabbed hold and wouldn't let go. The distraction of his steadily growing hard-on made him forget he should be easing into a proposal like the one he had in mind. Instead, it burst out of his mouth unchecked. "Are you forgiving enough to give me another shot?"

Chapter Six

Lana was certain she couldn't have heard him correctly. "I beg your pardon?"

"I want another shot at it."

"At...*it?*"

"Yes...*it.*" His gaze swept over her face, down her neck to the top of her blouse. "You should know I can do a hell of a lot better than I did the other night. I'd like to clear the blemish from my record."

The air conditioning did little to stop Lana's temperature from rising. "First I was a mistake, now I'm a *blemish?*"

"I never said *you* were a blemish... Shit. Why do women always twist words?"

She couldn't believe he had the nerve to look frustrated. Lana shot out of her chair. "It's pretty hard to twist those words, Brody. You think I care about your record? You think it's flattering to be the only notch on your bedpost you want another chance to nail?"

Brody stood too, so they were facing each other on opposite sides of the paper-littered desk. "This isn't about nailing you, Lana. Well"—that gaze flickered over her body again—"I do want that, but if you'd rather not go there, that's fine by me."

"I don't understand. You just said..."

"I know what I said." Pushing out a rough breath, Brody ran a hand over his face. Lana heard the rasp of his afternoon beard growth scraping against his palm and was transported back to the *Sunset*. His cheek brushing against hers, his breath in her ear, heated words no other man had ever uttered to her. Her blood already hot with annoyance, it wasn't much of a leap before desire made it catch fire.

She ought to walk out on him. He was too much trouble. Plying her with sweets and earnest apologies one minute, the next making her feel like a stain on his shirt. She'd waited three long years to get his attention for *this*?

"Look, I shouldn't have brought this up at work. It's not the right place to talk about it."

"I'm not sure there is a right place to discuss...whatever this is. But I'd never accuse you of sexual harassment, Brody." Her lips tilted at the thought. If he only knew of all the times she'd yearned for a little harassment of that nature from him.

"Thank God. Drew would kill me."

"I doubt it." Brody was obviously making a concerted effort to succeed at managing the restaurant and not a single employee had been able to fault his abilities as executive chef. He wasn't merely good at what he did, he was excellent, and when he asked someone to do something, the task was completed in short order. She knew Mick and the restaurant's two apprentices, Tyson and Paul, had a healthy respect for his instincts. "You're doing a good job, Brody."

He released a relieved breath. "Thanks. That means a lot, especially coming from you."

"Why especially coming from me?"

"Because so far I've done nothing but screw up with you. I'd like a chance to change that."

Lana tried to still the butterflies flapping around her

stomach. "You're talking about having s-sex with me again?"

He smiled a little at the way she stumbled over the S word. Why couldn't she at least pretend to be sophisticated? "What I want is to even the score. You didn't have an orgasm the other night, Lana, and I want to give you one. Sex is optional."

"I'm not sure I understand." But she was beginning to, and the images his words conjured made wet heat rush through her body. "I told you the other night that didn't matter, about the...orgasm."

"That's bullshit. If you'd ever had one you'd know that."

"Oh, I've had one." Lana blushed profusely when she realized what she'd unwittingly revealed. Thank God he couldn't know he was usually the man she fantasized about when she was enjoying herself on her own.

"Hell, Lana. You have a way of making me hot." He leaned his forearms on the computer monitor between them, bringing his face closer to hers. His eyes smoldered with devilish intentions and his words were a low thrum in his throat. "Next time, I want to be the one to make you come. I'll even keep my clothes on if you want because this is all about you. I can show you what it's like with a man instead of a..." Suddenly, he frowned. "Tell me you don't have one of those top-of-the-line models with all the rotating parts. Because I have to tell you, there are some things I can't do."

Lana stifled an embarrassed giggle when she realized what he was talking about. "I don't have a..." She couldn't even say the word vibrator in front of him. She flipped her hair and tried for a more cavalier expression. "I have seen them though. You know, on the Net."

He cocked a brow. "And you accuse me of visiting suspicious websites."

"What are you two up to?"

They both started and turned toward the doorway. Mick had his head stuck around the frame, his eyebrows raised as he looked from Brody to Lana.

"How come you're back?"

Lana almost jumped at Brody's surly tone, but Mick seemed unperturbed. "I forgot my smokes."

"Those things'll kill you, Jensen. Ever thought of trying the patches?"

Mick shrugged. "They're on my Christmas wish list. Are you two the only ones left?"

Lana fought to control her blush. Did he suspect something was going on? *Please God, tell me he didn't hear us talking about vibrators.* "Courtney's gone shopping, if that's what you're asking, Mick."

"Why would I be asking about Courtney?"

Lana's rolled her eyes. "You two are as bad as each other."

"Why?" Mick's baby blues brightened. "What did she say about me?"

"Nothing you want to hear." Lana laughed. "Are you looking for someone to hang out with? Because I'm done here." There was little point in going home to change out of her uniform now, only to put it back on in an hour.

"You're finished with the computer?"

Lana turned to see Brody scowling at her like she'd just stolen his favorite toy. "The new programs are all loaded. All you need to do is restart and everything should be fine."

"If it's not?"

Damn, but he could glower with the best of them. Lana felt her hackles prickling at his swift change in demeanor. "Then you might need to hire a professional technician. I can put you in touch with my guy if need be. Right now, I'm taking my break."

Grabbing her bag, Lana swept out of the office before Brody could think of a way to stop her. She had to escape the enclosed space because it overflowed with Brody's aura and wickedly erotic promises, so that thinking straight was impossible.

She spent her break with Mick and a couple of his mates at O'Ryan's Pub, where she drank lemonade and took a cursory interest in their epic game of pool. Much to Mick's dismay, she kept fumbling her shots, putting his twenty dollar bet in jeopardy. Lana's vision was too blinded by images of the things Brody might do to give her an orgasm while keeping his clothes on.

It was almost time to return to work when she caught sight of him. The pub's windows fronted onto Main Street and Brody strolled past on the opposite side of the road, hefting a large cardboard box of produce on one shoulder as though it weighed nothing and crunching on an apple he held in his other hand. His T-shirt rode up. She caught that glimpse of taut abdomen again, and it made all the muscles in hers bunch. As she stared, helpless to pull her admiring gaze from his casual strength, she was reminded of all the times she had watched him like this, unobserved and filled with longing. Wishing that once, just once, he would turn around, catch her eye and smile like he was happy to see her.

For three years she'd been disappointed, although come to think of it she had no clue what she'd expected. She'd never done a thing to solicit his attention because she'd been too crippled by the shyness that came along with her painful crush to converse with the kind of wit she wanted to. At the wedding she'd taken a risk, and while it may not have gone smoothly, she had gotten a better result than ever before. She'd managed to entice Brody into bed—who would have thought?

And now he wanted more. Brody Nash actually wanted more of her. It might only be a point of pride with him, but it had promising written all over it.

"Lana, you're up."

Reluctantly, Lana turned from the window and took the pool cue from Mick's grasp. "Already?"

"Hey, you're hardly one to poke fun at anyone else's pool playing. Your game hasn't been a roaring success so far."

"Let's see what I can do to change that."

Lana sank the next three balls, eliciting a round of whistles from the three men around her. "I think I have time to duck outside for a smoke after all." Mick pulled his lighter out of his shirt pocket.

"Brody's right, Mick," Lana told him. "You ought to try the patches."

Mick uttered an offended huff. "The two of *you* are as bad as each other," he pointed out, throwing what she'd said earlier about Courtney back at her.

As Mick sauntered out to the designated smoking area, Lana sank another ball and couldn't help but smile. She might not be as bad as Brody, but as a plan formulated in her mind, she figured there could be hope for her yet.

Brody liked his women experienced, Lana understood that. If she wanted to have a fling with a sex-with-no-strings kind of guy like him, all she had to do was put aside her feelings and act on a purely physical level. She simply needed to prove to him the sex meant nothing to her.

She could do that. Really.

Brody was on the deck servicing the *Sunset's* winch the following Monday when he glanced up and saw Lana striding along the wharf in his direction.

His heart slammed against his ribs. It had been three days since he'd made that outrageous and impulsive offer to be at her orgasmic service. *Three days*—not to mention three hot, sweaty and frustrating nights—during which she hadn't spoken a single word on the subject. And Brody hadn't felt he could broach it again. The whole manager-employee relationship they had going, temporary as it might be, rendered the idea of leaning on her for an answer out of the question. Besides, he'd made the offer. It was up to her to decide if she was going to take him up on it.

He couldn't help but be a little irked she'd taken three days to make a decision.

She came to a halt before him. She wore a T-shirt and a denim skirt that was pleasingly short, its hem frayed as if she'd ripped off the bottom half of it. Brody found he liked the image that conjured. She wore high platform clogs that made her legs go on forever and that shirt clung to her breasts, the white material transparent enough that he could see the outline of her bra. Nothing but plain white cotton, so it shouldn't have made his tongue stick to the roof of his mouth, but there was something about the way she looked today that shot her from cute, pretty territory into the stratosphere of knockout sexy.

"Hi there." Her jauntily issued greeting shook him out of an array of lewd thoughts. "Cat got your tongue?"

Nope. It's in perfect working order. Want to put it to good use? It took him a moment to get his voice to work. "You look amazing."

Her eyes sparkled in the morning light. "Thank you. Ditto to you."

Brody glanced down at his threadbare running shorts and faded chambray shirt, the buttons undone so the material hung sloppily off his shoulders. His hands were still covered in grease. By no stretch did he look *amazing*, and he figured maybe she was being ironic. "If I'd known you were coming, I would have cleaned up." He didn't like how much his statement revealed—to her as well as himself.

He cared if he looked good for her.

Don't get carried away. She's here for...what exactly? "You want to come aboard? I've got some fresh bread if you're hungry."

"I'd better not. I only need to talk for a minute."

Hope took a nosedive. She wasn't here to take him up on his offer. She'd come to tell him not now, not ever. Shit. "All right, Lana, I get it."

"Get what?"

His limbs felt heavy as he hauled himself over the stern and dropped onto the dock in front of her. The sexual frustration was probably going to be the death of him, but he couldn't say he faulted her decision. "I know a no when I hear one." He thought of saying *better luck next time*, but the idea of her searching for a sexual experience with someone else didn't sit comfortably in his mind.

He looked into her face, watching as the confusion in her pretty eyes cleared and her lips curved in a smile. Its effect was more dazzling than the high sun, and before Brody even knew what she was doing she stepped forward, wound her arms around his neck and kissed him.

Her lips were open and pliant. Wet and soft and so seductive he could only stand there and let the thrill of arousal open him up until she burrowed under his skin. He banded his forearms around her waist, trying to keep his hands off her so she wouldn't get grease all over her fresh white top. Her breasts nestled into the bare strip of skin between the open seams of his shirt, and he grew instantly hard as an iron bar against her abdomen.

When she pulled back Brody felt himself clinging a little. Up close, he saw that her lids were outlined with soft brown makeup, her lashes tinted dark. The taste of cherries on his tongue made him realize she'd been wearing lip-gloss too. The notion that she might have prettied herself up before she came to see him did something fluttery to his chest.

When she spoke her voice was thick and husky. "I came here to invite you to dinner."

Brody felt himself smiling. "Yeah?"

"But I have a problem. I can't cook for you. You're a professional and my specialty is two-minute noodles in a cup. I'd be much too embarrassed."

He swore, horrified. "You can't eat that stuff, Lana, it's not good for you. I can—"

"No," she cut him off. "I don't want you to cook because it's your night off and would probably seem like work to you. So that leaves us with takeaway, which in Graceville means pizza, Chinese or fish and chips. So it's one of those options or..." she took a deep breath, "...we could go out to dinner, unless you think that sounds too much like a date. I'm not trying to date you. I want to have sex with you—an affair. I need practice."

"Practice?"

"At some point I'll start dating again. It would be nice if I knew what I was doing by then."

"That's what you mean by practice?" He knew he sounded pissed off but couldn't seem to stop himself. This wasn't exactly what he had in mind when he offered her his services. "You want to polish the bedside manner for these other guys you want to date? Who are you talking about—Mick?"

"Mick?" She shook her head. "Haven't you worked out that he's infatuated with Courtney?"

All Brody knew for sure was that Mick Jensen always seemed to make Lana laugh, and that really bugged him. "So who are these other guys?"

"No one in particular. But you don't have a right to stop me from pursuing a relationship with a man who's willing to offer me one." She looked at him, her eyes steady. "It's not as if you want me for yourself."

Heat rose in his neck. "Ah, Lana, I..."

"Goodness, don't stammer, it doesn't suit you." She toyed with the lapel of his shirt. "I'm a mature woman, Brody, and I'd like to be treated as one. I don't want mixed messages between us. You can't act possessive if you're not willing to back it up."

Back it up? He'd like to back *her* up, against the nearest hard surface and prove to her she didn't want any other men. To hell with being considerate. He reached down and planted his hands on her ass, giving her cheeks a firm squeeze. Let her try and chat up some other guy when she had Brody-sized hand prints all over her butt.

He gleaned some satisfaction from the way she gasped at his maneuver, and took advantage of her surprise by sealing his lips over hers. He probed into her sassy mouth with his tongue, sweeping around in there like he owned the place. Knowing he had no rights to her was one thing, letting her think he would tolerate being one of many was another.

Wrestling with his male impulse to jump her delectable bones, Brody pulled out of the kiss, making sure this time she was the one clinging.

"Well, this is a frightfully public display of affection."

Brody almost groaned when he recognized the voice. Tearing his gaze away from the glazed desire in Lana's eyes, he frowned at Carol Buchanan as she approached. "Mrs. B, your timing is impeccable."

"I've always thought so. I'd say carry on but I'm not sure that would be wise. The poor girl's skirt might not make it." She turned her attention to Lana, inquiring as casually as can be. "Hello, Lana. How are you?"

"I'm, ah...good. Thank you, Mrs. Buchanan."

"Oh, why don't you call me Carol?"

Reluctantly Brody released Lana and allowed her to step out of their embrace. "Is there some reason you stopped by, Mrs. B?"

"I had to come over in person because you never have that mobile of yours turned on. I wanted to remind you about the barbeque today. You are still coming, aren't you?"

A pile of Drew's relatives had stayed on after the wedding to holiday in the area. Brody had promised he'd stop by and see everyone one more time before they left. "Wouldn't miss it," he said, although truth be told, he wished the lunch hadn't been today of all days, when he suddenly found himself with a wealth of more pleasurable options.

"Wonderful. You know a burger is never the same without your famous barbeque sauce, and Ray can't seem to make it as well as you do." She glanced at Lana. "You're welcome to come along too, Lana."

Brody sensed Lana's discomfort. "Oh no, I couldn't impose."

"It wouldn't be an imposition."

Lana persisted. "Really, I don't think I should."

"Oh, please do come," Carol beseeched in her cheerful

voice. "It's too lovely a day to be cooped up indoors, and there's always room at our table. Isn't that right, Brody?"

"It's true. She even feeds stray dogs." *And lonely kids.* There'd always been room at the Buchanan's table, in their house, for him. Brody glanced sidelong at Lana and saw she still appeared less than keen on attending lunch at the Buchanans'. He told Carol, "We'll talk about it," and tried not to notice how couple-like that sounded.

"All right then. I hope to see you both soon."

Once Carol had flitted back down the wharf in her ever-brisk manner, her silky ash-blonde bob glinting in the sunlight, Brody sought out Lana's gaze. "You've got something against barbeques?"

"Of course not. But I won't go."

"Why not?"

"If I go, Carol will think we're a couple."

"She already thinks we're a couple," Brody drawled. "You might as well get a decent meal out of it. If you wait while I get cleaned up, we can go together."

"Brody." Her serious tone stopped him before he could move toward the boat. "If you'd rather I didn't go, please say so. I know Carol put you in an awkward position and that family lunches are a very date-like event."

"And we're not dating, I get that." Did she have to keep spelling it out? "It's just a barbeque, Lana. What's the big deal?"

"I don't like to go anywhere I'm not welcome, that's all."

She folded her arms over her chest, and the defensiveness of the stance made him wonder who had made her feel unwanted. He also wondered whether it was too late to pop them on the nose. "Why?"

"I'm sensitive about that sort of thing I suppose because..."

She looked down at her feet, inordinately interested in her shoes. "My mother was forty-four when she had me, my father in his fifties. They already had two grown children and thought their parenting days were behind them. Instead of an early retirement, they had to start all over again. I always knew I'd been thrust upon them, that they hadn't really wanted me. I won't go where I'm not invited."

Brody felt a swift rise of anger. Lana shouldn't have had to go through that, not her. Smart, capable and self-sufficient, she was nobody's burden. Something inside him softened, morphed into a kind of kindred recognition he really didn't need. He shouldn't look for more ways in which they connected, but the commonality arced between them and hit him between the ribs. He knew what it felt like, being the kid nobody wanted.

He spoke with soft honesty. "*I'm* inviting you. I'd like you to be there."

Her smile was tremulous but hopeful. "Really?"

"Really." He tweaked her nose, leaving a smudge of grease behind. "I feel like I ought to keep you close by today. Time away from me might help you come to your senses."

"So that means you're agreeing to the...sex thing?"

The way she fumbled over the technicalities was exceedingly adorable. She really had no business making indecent propositions, just as he had no business taking her up on them. But he was only a man, a pretty easy lay at that. Some temptations were too difficult to resist. "Honey, if you walk up to any guy looking like you do today and tell him you want to use him for sex, you could probably get him to agree to anything."

She smiled. "I'll keep that in mind."

Suddenly Brody wished he could take his words back. The thought of her using the technique on someone else made his hands clench into fists. "I think you'd better head home and change first. I made a real mess of your skirt." Later, he was going to make a mess of everything else she was wearing as well. "Give me your address and I'll pick you up in half an hour."

Brody felt the grin splitting his face a few minutes later as he watched her leave, two black handprints on faded denim swinging from side to side as she walked away.

A little over half an hour later, Lana's heart jumped to her throat when she heard a car pull into the driveway of her duplex apartment. She'd changed into another skirt—a blue and white floral number that swirled around her thighs when she walked—and a fresh T-shirt in pale blue. Grabbing her handbag, she went outside to meet Brody. She hadn't had time to clean her apartment as she'd originally intended, and she didn't want him to see how cluttered with books and mismatched furniture it was. From what little she'd seen of his yacht, he seemed to lean toward neatness and order.

He met her halfway to her door. The appreciative look he blazed over her had her insides humming. "Are all your skirts that short?"

She passed her eyes over his fresh clothes. "Are all your shirts that black?"

"Not all of them. There's no law against black."

"No law against short, either," Lana pointed out as she allowed him to hand her into the passenger seat of his car.

He stood in the open door for a long moment, blatantly ogling her legs. "There ought to be. I'm very distracted right now, driving might be dangerous. Sure you don't want to ditch this party and get started on dinner?"

She'd like nothing better, and her pulse leapt at his suggestion. But she said, "Carol would be devastated."

Issuing a disgruntled noise, he closed her door and headed around to the driver's side.

As Brody took the coast road that wound its way around the cliff side and kept the blue waters of the Pacific on their right as they headed north, Lana admired the immaculately kept interior of the 1970s-style Ford. "You love this car," she observed.

He smiled. "She's a beauty."

"It's so well cared for. What do you do with it while you're away?" Her query sobered Lana somewhat, reminding her as it did of his long-established habit of leaving Graceville for months at a time. *Don't forget, Lana, he always leaves.*

But he was here now, and she had every intention of making the most of it. She was going to have an affair with Brody. At the moment that was all that mattered.

"Ray keeps it in his garage," he answered. "He helped me restore it a few years back. Loves it as much as I do."

"He's like a father to you, isn't he?"

A laugh barked out of him, sharp and bitter. "No. Ray actually seems to like me."

The tightness of his voice gave Lana the message that his father was off limits as a topic of conversation. But after a few tense moments he added, "Let's just say dear old dad and I weren't the best of buddies. He died three years ago, liver disease. He did like to drink, so I guess everything bites you on the ass eventually."

"I suppose so," Lana agreed quietly. "What about your

mother? Is she still around?"

"Nope."

From the implacable lines of his profile she deduced that subject wasn't up for discussion either. "I'm sorry. I didn't mean to pry."

"I don't like to look back, Lana," he told her. "I haven't seen my mother in twenty years. There's no story there."

No story he was willing to tell, not her anyway. When she'd decided to start this thing, she'd known Brody wasn't an open book. Why had she thought their agreeing to a sexual liaison would change that?

The Buchanan's house was an older style two-story brick-veneer dwelling in a quiet cul-de-sac. The garden overflowed with vibrant petunias, daisy bushes and marigolds that waved jauntily in the soft breeze, as though greeting them. Parking in the street, Brody gestured for her to precede him as he bypassed the front door in favor of a path that led around the side of the house.

The yard was filled with people, and for a moment Lana was taken aback. A barbeque at her parents' house had consisted of the two of them and Lana, with the occasional inclusion of one of the much older brothers who she rarely saw or her Aunt Mabel, her mother's sister. They hadn't exactly been party animals. As a result, large gatherings had the power to intimidate her.

"I'm so glad you came." Carol Buchanan approached and surprised Lana by giving her a quick peck on the cheek. As if she were a part of this family. The nice sensation of inclusion unsettled Lana. She couldn't afford to get attached to any of these people because today was likely the only time she would visit this house.

But Carol didn't treat her like an interloper as she took her around and introduced her to everyone as Brody's "friend"—air quotes practically visible. Drew's sisters and various aunts responded with assumptions Lana couldn't get them to change no matter how many disclaimers she gave.

Someone put a glass of wine in her hand, and Lana drank it to keep from going hoarse from all the small talk. Drew's sister Deanne was a nurse who lived in Wollongong with her husband and two children, while the eldest Buchanan, Belinda, was divorced and worked as a store manager in Melbourne. Lana started to lose track of who was who after a while. She stuffed her face on crackers and Brie cheese, and ended up talking computer games with a nice guy named Daniel who'd introduced himself as Drew's cousin.

Not long after she and Daniel began getting to know each other, she felt the warm weight of Brody's hand settling on her waist. His touch made her skin tingle, while the steely tone of his voice startled her. "How you doing there, Danny?" He didn't ask it in a conversational way, like he was actually interested. He demanded in more of a *what the hell do you think you're up to* manner that made Daniel back up so far he ran into an Esky, making the ice and drinks inside clink together.

Daniel muttered a reply, flushed violently and was gone before Lana could utter a shocked goodbye.

"Could you help me in the kitchen for a second?" Brody asked. She was being swept inside before she could sputter an answer. In the middle of the blue and white tiled kitchen, Brody pointed to the stove. "Mind stirring that for me?"

Lana parked her hands on her hips and glared at him. "Is that an order or a request?"

His grin appeared, faintly apologetic. "Can you please make sure that doesn't stick to the bottom of the pan while I make the bruschetta?"

Bruschetta did sound nice, so Lana picked up the wooden spoon and began stirring the concoction simmering on the stove. She inhaled the sweet onion fragrance. "Your famous barbeque sauce?"

"That's it."

They worked together in silence for a few moments. Brody chopped fresh herbs with such a swift action that if she hadn't known his occupation she would have feared for his fingers. After a moment Lana ventured to ask, "Are you going to tell me what that was about outside?"

"What what was about?" he inquired, entirely innocent.

Brody innocent. What a ludicrous idea. "You scared the life out of Daniel and nearly dragged me inside. Is he a serial killer or something?"

"He's twenty-two and horny as a toad." He flicked her a look. "And he was checking out your rack."

Lana couldn't help it. She laughed so hard she almost dropped the spoon. "Brody, I do not have a *rack*." She glanced down at her decidedly flat chest. "Believe me, guys do not *check me out*."

"I'm not a guy?" His gaze swept over her, more scorching than the sauce bubbling on the hotplate.

"Present company excepted." But how long was that aberration going to last? How long was gawky Lana Green going to be able to keep Brody interested? She'd spent three days dying, waxing, scrubbing and buying sexy-heeled shoes, but those things could only take her so far.

"If you must know, Daniel and I were talking about Warcraft." Lana changed the subject swiftly, before the notion of the inevitable end of her affair with Brody depressed her again. "It's an online computer game. Being into Warcraft is tantamount to being captain of the chess club. I'm a *nerd*,

Brody. In school I tinkered with computers and watched *Star Trek* and didn't know how to talk to the cute boys. The guys who wanted to hang out with me were geeks too, more interested in their laptops than trying to get me into the back seat of a car."

"Is that why you were still a virgin?" he asked, his voice soft with disbelief. "No one even tried to sleep with you?"

She avoided reminding him he'd never tried to sleep with her until a week ago, and even then she'd had to throw herself at him to get his attention. "I never got past the kissing stage with anyone in high school. I met someone serious when I was eighteen—Mark Sumner. His parents were even more conservative than mine and he'd been brought up to believe sex before marriage was a sin, so we just didn't go there because it freaked him out so much. He asked me to marry him, but I was twenty years old."

Lana shrugged. She'd been very fond of Mark but she hadn't been in love with him. She hadn't even been that disappointed when he didn't want to have sex with her—a little disheartened by her inability to turn him to temptation but it wasn't as if she'd known how. It wasn't as though she had knockers the size of grapefruit to blind a man to his better intentions. "So I guess that's why I never slept with anyone until you."

Embarrassed by her admissions, Lana whirled around and made painstaking work of stirring the sauce. Why did she have to say all that? She wanted so much to seem worldly and brazen, but despite all her intentions she ended up acting like...herself. She'd never been very good at being something she was not.

All the external changes she'd made suddenly seemed pointless. She was never going to be mistaken for a femme fatal, no matter what she did. Brody was going to get bored so fast this fling would be over before it began.

"So what are you saying?" Brody asked at last, his voice taut. "That you want one of these geeky types, someone to play computer games with? Someone like Daniel. Is there an IQ test he needs to take? Because maybe you ought to warn him, so he can study."

"What *are* you talking about?" Lana frowned at him. "I was not trying to pick up Daniel."

"Are you sure? Don't let me cramp your style. He's going back to Sydney tomorrow. If you want to make a move you'd better do it now."

"You're being a jerk. I told you at the marina that you had no right to stop me seeing other men." There hadn't been a spark of attraction between her and Drew's cousin, but Lana felt the need to reiterate her position. "So if I *did* want to exchange phone numbers with Daniel you wouldn't be able to stop me."

"Is that right?" He took a couple of steps toward her and shivers raced up and down Lana's spine. She backed up instinctively and bumped the kitchen counter. Brody placed a hand on either side of her, trapping her with his body heat. "I won't be made to look like an idiot so you can shop around. We might not be dating, but as long as these people think we are, you might want to act like it."

"If I didn't know better I'd say you were jealous." Lana's heart did a crazy little flip at the thought, which reminded her exactly why she'd asked for there to be no mixed messages between them. She couldn't afford to see more in their affair than what was there, it was too much risk for her heart. "Or are you just being an alpha dog, marking your favorite tree so the other dogs will know it's yours—for as long as *you* want it to be.

I'm not a Eucalyptus, you know."

"I know. You're a damned frustrating woman."

"Why? Because I won't let you boss me around? I've seen you at the restaurant. You like to give orders."

He moved a little closer until his chest brushed against hers, causing her breasts to tingle, the tips to draw into stiff peaks. His voice dropped to a sexy rumble, and his smile hinted at a world of erotic possibility, "You don't know the half of it yet."

Chapter Seven

A moment later Deanne came in to ask after the sauce. Brody backed off to busy himself pouring it from the saucepan into a bowl, leaving Lana to wonder exactly what he'd meant by his last comment. She brushed a tendril of hair behind her ear, and her cheek felt hot to the touch.

Drew's sister watched Brody's meticulous actions with a small shake of her head before turning to Lana. "Can you believe this all started because my dad got him a job washing dishes just to keep him off the streets at night?"

"Deanne, no one wants to hear that story."

Deanne ignored Brody's warning tone. "Lana probably does. Come with me, Lana," Deanne suggested with a defiant glance in Brody's direction. "I'll tell you anything you want to know about him."

Deanne led her to the long table underneath the pergola in the backyard and ushered her into a seat. Someone handed her a plate and she proceeded to pile it with hamburger fixings and a side of potato salad. Throughout the meal, Deanne regaled Lana with tales of Brody's youthful exploits, including an incident where he was caught trying to steal a bottle of peach schnapps from O'Ryan's Pub to impress a girl. He'd been lucky to escape without legal charges, and the event had led to his stint as a professional dishwasher.

"God I hated that job," Brody groused. "I did it for a year before I was put on as an apprentice when Drew was hired. Pat O'Ryan was a cranky old bastard."

"Taught you everything you know, did he?"

Brody seemed surprised, but not displeased by Lana's sassy remark. "Hey, I'm not old."

Lana didn't think he was a bastard either, and his tendency to get cranky didn't seem as intimidating as it once had. In fact she thought he was...

Her heart kicked her in the chest. She thought he was wonderful. He took Drew's sisters' endless teasing in stoic stride and was unfailingly respectful toward Mrs. Buchanan and all the assorted relatives. He put up with it when Ray Buchanan reached over and ruffled his hair like he was ten years old, and listened with suitable animation when Drew's nine-year-old nephew told him in scrupulous detail about the bream he'd caught when his grandfather had taken him fishing.

And he'd been so sweet back at the marina when she'd spilled out all that stuff about her parents, unwittingly revealing what a lonely child she'd been. In bringing her here, he'd counteracted those old insecurities and made her feel wanted. His dubious past rabble-rousing aside, Lana thought Brody had grown into a decent man, a man she desired in more than the physical sense.

Oh God. I'm so stupid. She couldn't believe she'd thought she *might* be risking her heart by getting in deeper with Brody. Her heart had already gone bye-bye—she'd lost it three years ago in the kitchen at the Grill when Drew had introduced her to the other chefs. She'd barely been able to utter a greeting, she'd been so overcome with the sense that the man standing before her was The One. The man of her dreams, her knight in shining armor, the most desirable specimen of manhood she'd ever laid eyes on. Over the years she'd convinced herself she'd imagined the intensity of that meeting, that love unrequited wasn't love but a childish infatuation, the futile human impulse to covet what was out of reach.

All logical arguments that didn't do a darn thing to change how Lana felt. She loved him. She always had and she feared she always would, even though he would never return those feelings.

Never?

Around her, conversations carried on, rapid-fire dialogue exchanged over food and wine. For Lana, it was difficult to concentrate on chitchat because right there in the Buchanans' shady suburban backyard, her life was changing.

For twenty-three years she'd sat back and let things happen to her—or not happen as the case may be. She'd tiptoed around her parents' vexation at having been surprised with a child when they least expected it. She'd sat by as boy after boy passed her over in favor of something else because they hadn't found her attractive enough to hold their interest, and instead of doing something about that, she'd let their disregard define her self-image. She'd fallen into her job as a waitress when she needed money to buy her first car and do the computer courses she'd wanted to do. She liked the job, but she hadn't chosen it.

Life had happened *to* her, not because of her. The only time she'd stepped out of her comfort zone and changed that was the night of Drew and Sidney's wedding, when she'd chanced flirting with Brody. Look where that had gotten her. She was here with him on a beautiful sunny day, meeting the people who considered him family, making him jealous, making him want her. Who knew what else she might be able to achieve if she set her mind to it?

Never say never, Lana.

Her mood improved in direct counterpoint to Brody's as the afternoon wore on. She greedily accepted a second helping of potato salad—Brody scowled. She said yes to mango cheesecake and coffee—Brody's foot nudged hers under the table with pointed force. She caught his eye and interpreted the hot look. *Time to go*, it said. Lana smiled and drank her coffee, delighting in the fact he couldn't wait to get her alone. When she agreed to go inside and look at Carol's collection of heirloom quilts, Brody cut her a look that seethed with impatience. By the time they left, it was after four o'clock and Brody nearly dragged her to the car.

As he settled behind the wheel and gunned the engine, Lana remarked, "Well, that bordered on rude."

"You were doing that on purpose." Shifting the car into gear, Brody pulled out into the street.

"What? Carol has a wonderful array of quilts. You should see the stitching."

"Stitching," Brody groused. He cast a glance at her as he made a right turn, and his lips kicked up in a way that sent shivers rippling through her. "You'll keep."

"Oh? What are you planning on doing with me?"

"Wait and see." He returned his gaze to the road. After a moment he said, "You know, I haven't been able to get our conversation out of my head."

"Which conversation is that?"

"In the office the other day." His voice dropped an octave. "I haven't stopped thinking about how you must look when you get yourself off."

His words shocked her, had her shifting in her seat with both embarrassment and arousal. What would he think if he knew she'd done that in his bed while she waited for him? "That, um...interests you?"

"Hell yes."

"You know I..." Lana glanced out the passenger window, watching lush green grass and sapphire blue ocean pass by. If she was going to have a chance with Brody, she would have to do things she'd never done, be braver than she'd ever been. She took a deep breath. "That night on your boat. I did that while I was waiting for you."

He was silent for what felt like a full minute. When at last he spoke his voice was hoarse. "Are you trying to make me crash this car?"

Lana giggled, nervousness spilling out of her. "No. Merely making conversation."

"I love your idea of banter."

"I try to be entertaining."

"So entertain me."

His casual suggestion was underpinned by steely demand. "You mean..."

"Your place is still ten minutes away and I'm not known for my patience."

She laughed. "I can't do that."

"That's not what you just told me."

Lana crossed her arms over her chest, turning to send him a challenging look. She couldn't believe they were debating the merits of her masturbating in the front seat of his car, or that she was having so much fun while she was at it. "I'm sick of doing *that.* That's why I got you."

"You think *you* got *me*?"

"Didn't I?"

She could almost hear him thinking about it. After a moment he sank back against the car's bench seat. "Shit. I was seduced."

"Are you complaining?"

"No. I'm just amazed how much front you have for a novice."

Although the sun had dipped behind a cloud, Lana felt warmth shine on her at the note of admiration she heard in his voice. "I'm learning all the time."

"Don't be such a know-all." He flashed her a smile that told her she could be anything she wanted. "From here on in, I take over. You got that? I'm going to teach you stuff that will make your toes curl, but you have to take orders from me."

That was exactly the arrogant attitude that should get her back up. It didn't happen. Her back was decidedly relaxed about the whole thing, while other parts of her fired to life at Brody's proclamation. Lana tried for a protest but it was weak. Shamefully, wantonly weak. "I feel like I should object."

"You won't." That smile reappeared. "Take off your panties."

She could refuse if she really wanted to. Brody didn't mean he was going to give her *orders* exactly, at least she didn't think so. She lacked experience, not knowledge. This was some kind of risqué game. The question was, could she play it?

"Come on." He reached over and ran his hand up her leg, from her knee to the hem of her skirt. Moist heat pooled at his light touch. "I'll make it worth your while."

Good Lord, she couldn't do this. But as though her brain no longer had much control over her actions, Lana found herself relenting. With a wiggle and a shimmy, she shucked her lacy-edged underwear, leaving them on the floor by her feet.

Brody expelled a breath, and she wondered if he'd expected her to chicken out. His reaction made it easier for her to follow his instructions. He touched her thigh again. "Open your legs."

Heart pounding in her throat, Lana did as he said. The air

in the car was warm, but it felt cool against her bare flesh. It was unbelievably wicked, not wearing underwear in the middle of the afternoon in a moving car.

Brody's hand slipped beneath her skirt. Lana's heart stilled as he neared her naked lips, flat-out stopped when his fingers danced over them. Wetness gathered, generating more heat. He caressed her folds until they unfurled, presenting her eager nub for his inspection. Brody slid his thumb over it and buried his middle finger inside her at the same time, the duel sensations causing Lana to arch off the seat into his hand.

He kept up the delicious motion while his other hand gripped the steering wheel, guiding the car as effortlessly as though his attention wasn't arrested elsewhere. She knew he wasn't as stoic as he appeared—she could sense the increased rapidity of his breathing—but there was something incredibly exciting about his air of unshaken control. This was the something about Brody that had always thrilled her, even scared her a little. The sense that he could make her do things, feel things, far beyond her experience without ever breaking a sweat.

"You like that?" he asked, almost conversationally.

"Hmm." She closed her eyes, not quite up to doing this with them wide open. He wiggled his finger and her head dropped back against the seat.

"Feels nice, doesn't it? My finger inside you, my thumb rubbing your tight little clit."

She would have told him he sounded smug, but he had her approaching ecstasy literally in his hand. Perhaps he had a right to be smug. "Yes."

"Is this how you do it?"

"Usually," she squeaked, as he rubbed a soft little circle over her clit.

"In the bath?" he asked, blithely inserting a second finger into her wet channel. "In bed?"

"Both." Lana rocked into his hand, undulating to the motion he set with his stroking fingers. The pressure built inside her, a tightening of her womb that grew steadily in force.

His voice epitomized self-satisfaction. "In *my* bed."

"Brody..." Lana rotated her hips, seeking added pressure, deeper penetration. So close to the edge she could see it looming ahead.

"It's not far now."

"I know!"

He chuckled. "All right, we'll finish this off here." Pressing the heel of his hand down on her mound, Brody thrust his fingers deeper inside her, plunging them in and out with a marauding force that was so much more powerful, so much *better* than anything she had ever done on her own, that Lana cried out and pushed back, rocking, rocking until it hit her in a rush. A powerful climax, like a blustering wind, that carried her away into heat and joyous light.

After a moment, Brody removed his hand. Dazed, Lana watched him operate the column shift as he turned into her street, and couldn't believe those capable fingers had been inside her an instant ago. Neither could she believe she'd let him do that to her in broad daylight, in his car. It had been the most exciting, outrageous, *shameless* thing she'd ever done.

He parked in the driveway of her duplex and killed the engine. Lana unlatched her seatbelt. "I suppose 'thank you for the ride' is appropriate."

She heard the awkward lilt in her voice and so did Brody. "Don't be embarrassed."

"I can't help it. I got carried away."

"So did I." Placing an arm around her shoulders he drew her across the seat so she was at his side. He chucked her under the chin until she raised her eyes. His were full to the brim with stormy desire and a healthy dose of approval. "You're so damned sexy."

Lana smiled at his praise. "For a novice?"

He shook his head. "Not just for a novice."

She climbed out of the car on shaky legs and led the way to her door. The instant she opened it and stepped over the threshold, Brody snaked an arm around her waist and pulled her back against him. She felt the tension shaking his body. The door slammed as he kicked it shut. "Turn around."

The fire in his eyes burned her skin, made the wild experience in the car seem like little more than a prelude. When he swept forward and kissed her, she met his lips with hungry purpose, drowning in him, until he growled against her mouth. "Legs. Around me. *Now*."

Winding her legs around his waist, Lana gave breathless directions to her bedroom between hungry kisses. He carried her there effortlessly, thrilling Lana with his easy masculine strength, making her feel feminine in a way she never had. Her quilt was cool and soft at her back, a stark contrast to the hard heat of Brody's body as it pressed her down into the fabric. He kissed her until her lips were swollen and raw. Then he went to work on her neck, nipping at her flesh until Lana responded with a whimper of shocked delight that he swallowed when he once again took her mouth.

The impatience was steadily mounting in her body. She tugged on his shoulders, trying to pull him closer. "Touch me."

"I will, believe me." He slipped his hands beneath her T-shirt, kept sliding his touch up her arms until the garment disappeared. He gazed for a moment at her skimpy white bra, holding her wrists against the pillow above her while he traced its outline with an exploratory finger. "I didn't spend enough time on this that night on the boat. Undressing you, looking at you. I can't believe how beautiful you are."

"You don't have to charm me," Lana remarked wryly. "I'm already in bed with you."

Something soft tempered the lustful intentions written all over his face. He looked steadily into her eyes. "Those guys you knew were idiots. *I* was an idiot for three years, for not seeing what was right in front of me." He lifted a lock of her hair and brought it to his nose, inhaling its scent. "I love your hair."

"It's not really red, remember?"

"It's soft and smells like apples." Slowly, he moved his fingers to the front clasp of her bra and deftly popped it open. Never tearing his gaze from hers, he covered one of her breasts with his hand, tenderly rotating his palm over it until the crest hardened. "You have such pretty breasts."

Caught somewhere between embarrassment and pleasure, Lana almost laughed. "There's not much there to admire."

He flicked the tip of his finger over her nipple and it leapt in excited response. "I admire their enthusiasm."

"Well, I guess that's something."

He grinned. "Lana, honey, that's everything." While he continued softly massaging her breasts, he linked the fingers of his other hand through one of hers and guided it toward the bed head. He curled her grip around one of the wrought-iron bars. "Hold on to that with both hands. Don't let go unless I tell you to."

"Is that another order?"

"Yep." Watching her face, he brushed his fingers over her nipples, then took one between his thumb and forefinger and gave it a light tug.

Gasping at the sharp sensation, Lana tried to pull away. Something made her hold on to the headboard though, as Brody had instructed. Immediately he softened his touch, caressing her flesh before dipping his head and swirling his tongue around it.

Pleasure slid through her, mounting into frustration as he kept his ministrations achingly gentle. Lana writhed on the bed. When he once again gripped her nipple and tugged firmly, the sharp sensation was accompanied by an intensifying of the ache between her legs. Dampness pumped from her core onto her thighs.

As though he knew, Brody touched her there, collecting the moisture on his fingers and touching it to her enlarged clit. "A good hurt?"

She nodded mutely, holding Brody's dark gaze as he performed the same action with her other breast. His callused fingers rasped against her sensitive nipples, his tongue always soothing the soft abrasion before his teeth gently tugged. When the sensations began to overwhelm her, Lana let go of the headboard and tried to reach for him.

"Ah-ah. I told you not to do that, sweetness," he admonished. When he rose to his knees above her he appeared big, dominating and thrillingly dangerous. He began unbuckling his belt. "Do I have to take more drastic measures?"

Lana's throat went dry as his meaning began to sink in. Would he go so far as to tie her up? Her pulse accelerated out of control. "Is this where you turn into the big bad pirate and kidnap the innocent general's daughter to use her as a love slave?"

His dark brows formed surprised curves. "Do you want it to be?"

God, did she? Like anyone else, she'd had fantasies. Abduction by a sexy pirate was an old favorite, but Lana had never thought for a minute she might live something like that out.

Brody smiled at her hesitation, running the belt over her stomach, her breasts. The tactile pleasure made her nipples draw tighter. Brody let out a soft groan and reached out to tweak one. "I'd never do anything you didn't want to do."

Realizing he wasn't going to force the issue made her feel safer with him. She said, "That's not your reputation, Captain."

His brows hiked again, his lips twitching. "I wasn't aware I had a reputation."

"Oh, you do. People warned me about you. They said if ever I got into your clutches I'd be very, very sorry."

"That's rude of people, not giving a man a chance to redeem himself. You shouldn't have listened." He held her wrists against the bed head and began looping the belt around them. "Now I'll have to keep you here a while, until you admit they're all wrong."

Lana's heart thundered. It amazed her that she was doing this, and she couldn't contain the buzz dancing through her. "I'll never admit that."

"You will." He pulled the belt tight, strapping her securely to the wrought iron. His gaze passed over her face and for a moment Lana could swear he really was a rogue with nothing but wicked intentions. "When I'm finished with you. Until your ransom is paid, you're mine to do with as I wish."

Locating the zip of her skirt, Brody parted it and slid the garment down her legs. His touch on her bared flesh was confident, peremptory. "You have a very nice pussy. I'm going to enjoy using it, pleasuring it. I'm going to make you scream for me."

Lana had to bite her lip to stop a moan escaping. "I'll never let you touch me." Her voice was not nearly as strident as she'd aimed for.

"Why not? Has a man never touched you here?"

"Of course not." She strove for indignant affront. "I'm as pure as fresh snow."

He laughed softly, tracing his finger around her plump, juicy folds. "Not from where I'm sitting. Your legs are spread so wide you're practically begging me to taste your sweet lips. Beg me, little one. Beg the nasty pirate to touch you and I'll be gentle."

"Never."

He stopped her attempt to clamp her thighs shut, instead pushing them farther open and holding them securely to the bed. "Now, now. You don't want me to have to tie your legs down too—or do you?"

The very thought made her core heat. Dear Lord, she'd let him do that in a heartbeat. But not this time. Now, she was too impatient to know the sensation of his mouth on her. "No, please don't. I promise I'll be good."

"Oh, I know you will. It's going to be *so* good, using you every which way I want, while you can't do a thing to stop me. I'm going to show you how good it feels to be at a man's service, little one."

His high-handed performance was making Lana impossibly wet, her arousal fuelled by the thought that she wasn't sure how much of it was really an act, and how much was pure Brody. He fisted the shirt at his back and hauled it over his head. The sight of his bare chest alone, so strong and wide and peppered with silky black hair, had the need inside her bunching tight, ready to implode. When he stood and took off his pants too, she knew her cream seeped out of her onto the sheets.

He settled on his knees between her legs and inserted a broad finger inside her slick channel. Lana bucked against the pleasure. "You see? Already you're enjoying the way I touch you."

"No, I'm only doing this because you..." she undulated helplessly against the seductive rhythm of his finger, "...because you give me no choice."

He leaned over her, his lips brushing against her ear. "You secretly like having your choice taken away though, don't you? It's all pleasure and no guilt. You can enjoy this, and later deny that you did, that you're the kind of woman who would lay herself open for a reprobate like me and love it." He inserted another finger into her with an insolent plunge. "Love every lusty..." his tongue flicked out and licked at her earlobe, "...fulfilling..." with his thumb, he applied pressure to her clit, making her arch and gasp, "...second of it."

"Oh God. Please. *Please.*"

"What are you asking me for? You want to know what it's like to have a hungry pirate feast on your hot, tasty pussy?"

Lana's hips surged as though in answer, even as she rasped, "No. Don't."

He merely smiled. "Liar."

Slipping down her body, he settled himself between her parted thighs. Finding the moist core of her, he ran his tongue around the entrance, lightly. Lana hadn't expected such heat and softness, hadn't realized how natural it would feel. She gasped in surprised delight when he repeated the maneuver, rotating her hips in an instinctive move that encouraged him to touch that sleek wet tongue to the burning knot of flesh between her lips, to bury it fully into her channel.

He denied her that when he lifted his head. "You've never

had a man's mouth between your legs before, I can tell. Is it what you expected?"

"No," she breathed. "I mean, I've never imagined such scandalous behavior."

His soft laugh brushed air over her sensitive folds. "I bet you have. I'd wager you've thought about it a lot and that you've secretly longed to be bound just like this, forced to submit to the pleasure you pretend not to want. That you've had forbidden fantasies about someone like me doing this to you."

He parted her flesh with his fingers and tickled her clitoris with his fast flicking tongue. Lana bucked against his arms where they held her thighs to the bed. He only gave her as much as he wanted to, enough to make her quiver and pulse against his tongue, before he drew back and blew a warm soft breath over her flesh. Lana cried out and tugged on the belt securing her wrists, wishing she could thread her fingers through his midnight hair and hold his face against her.

"Hmm, you taste delicious, little one. Fresh and sweet. I could do this all night."

"No!" She'd die if he tortured her for that long. She'd never imagined she could be this excited. Her nipples were hard and distended, her vagina clamped down on the emptiness inside her, begging for something to fill it. "Please, end it now."

"There's only one way to end it, and you still say you don't want it."

"No, I want it. Please, Brody, I need to come."

"Hey, what happened to Captain?"

"It was a stupid idea. I can't pretend not to like this."

"Ah, sweetness. You're way too honest." He licked around the outer rim of her entrance before inserting a thick finger inside her. "Is this what you want?"

"Yes. And more of your mouth on me."

He muttered what sounded like an epithet before lowering his head and taking her clit gently into his mouth. He sucked on it softly, while moving his finger in and out of her in a lazy rhythm that hypnotized her, had her body writhing against the mattress in a sensuous motion. She relaxed her thighs, the tension moving from her limbs to the taut gathering ball in her abdomen that seemed linked to Brody's tongue by an invisible string. It tightened to a knot as he licked her, began to spin out of control as he moved his finger faster, deeper inside her.

When he added a second finger to the first, Lana unraveled. She undulated against him, gasping in stunned satisfaction as he sucked her clit and pumped his fingers in and out of her pussy, taking her to a climax that made her forget who she was.

As she came down from that great height, Lana knew *whose* she was. She was his. It was irrevocable, the knowledge bringing both a sense of completion and utter, heart-pounding terror. She loved him without reservation, and when he let her go it wouldn't merely hurt, it would devastate.

If he lets you go. Think positive, Lana. She detected the tremor in his hand as it stroked along her thigh, sensed the tenderness in the way he spread kisses over her stomach and knew he hadn't been completely unaffected by what had just happened. She let herself hope it meant something, that his own satisfaction when it came would touch him on more than a physical level, as hers had.

"Brody, I want you inside me." And she wanted him to lose control too.

"You're sure?"

"Do I have to ask twice?"

"Hell no. Let me get my wallet."

"Look in my top drawer."

He pulled out the box of condoms she'd gone to the next town to buy. He raised his eyebrows at the label. "Chocolate?"

Lana felt herself blush. Trussed up naked on her bed and she was blushing about condoms. "I thought it was appropriate."

He shook his head and smiled at her as he slid one over his erection. Then he was above her, his strong arms corded as he braced himself on the bed. Her muscles, still trembling with aftershocks, rippled with pleasure when his solid cock breached her entrance. She wrapped her legs around his hips, trying to draw him farther into her body, but he held back. She knew what he was doing and said, "There's no pain."

He pushed in a little more. "I didn't like hurting you last time."

She arched her hips. "I can take it."

With a groan he sank in to the hilt. This time the extension of her muscles was glorious, like the first stretch in the morning after a particularly agreeable sleep. His body fulfilled her, found her feminine mysteries and solved them.

"Let me touch you." She strained against the bonds. "Please."

"Nah. You said you can take it, so lie there and take it like a woman."

Lana laughed at his outrageous statement, and after a moment Brody joined in, the combined vibrations doing weird and wonderful things to the place where they were joined. "How do women usually take it, Brody?"

He smiled, full of devilish knowledge. "Loudly."

He started a steady, delicious motion that turned Lana's laughter to gasping sighs. She looked into his dark eyes, the predatory gleam there exciting her. She still wished she could hold him but this way was unexpectedly nice too. He could try whatever he wanted when she was bound, and Lana didn't think there was anything Brody Nash could do that she wouldn't like.

After a while Brody slowed the motion of his hips, frustrating her again. "Think you can come again, sweetness?"

"No."

"Wrong answer."

He hit a nerve when he tilted his pelvis, accompanying the move with a full, deep thrust that made Lana gasp. The tight heat began to build again in her womb. "Maybe...if you keep doing—oh God, that."

Lana gripped the headboard above her and held on for dear life as he found her with his fingers and prodded her toward another release. His patience was unshakeable and the pace of his thrusts didn't pick up until her breathing became shallow, and the humming began to permeate her body, zeroing in on the place where he breached her delicate flesh.

She didn't feel delicate, she felt strong in the way primitive creatures were—all instinct and physiology and drive. Lana kept her gaze on his, felt his eyes penetrating hers in a mirroring of his body's possession. She saw it the moment he met her in the wilds. His face changed, his expression turning grim with intent and raw need as he took her harder, faster. Watching Brody come undone before her eyes touched something deep in Lana that set off her climax. She roared in utter joy as he pounded into her and unleashed himself.

As she rode the downward slope from orgasmic heaven, Lana made an oath. She told herself she could do this—be his dream girl, his fantasy come true. She was going to throw all she had at him until he admitted he didn't want to lose her. Right then, when they were joined in the most intimate manner possible, Lana vowed she was going to make Brody Nash love her if it was the last thing she ever did.

Chapter Eight

As her breathing slowly normalized, Lana felt the slight tingle in her fingers, the weightless ache in her arms. "Brody? Could you untie me now?"

Muttering a hasty apology, he reached above her and slipped the belt from around her wrists. Taking her hands in his, he rubbed at her pulse points until her circulation flowed freely again. His brows furrowed with concern. "I wasn't too rough on you, was I?"

Lana smiled her answer, knowing she must look like the Queen of Sheba after she'd just had every last one of her demands met. "No."

He rolled onto his back, taking her along so she lay sprawled on top of him. He touched her face and smiled softly. "You surprised the hell out of me with that pirate stuff."

She laughed and blushed at the same time. "You recovered pretty quickly."

"Anything to please a lady." He twirled her hair around his finger. "You have a lot of fantasies, Lana?"

"Self-pleasure is the only sex I've had up till recently. You have to do something to make it interesting."

"I get the feeling I'm going to have trouble keeping up with you."

"Why? Don't you have fantasies?"

When he didn't answer, Lana lifted her head, linking her hands on his chest and resting her chin on them. There was something unreadable but unmistakably carnal in his dark eyes as he stared at her. He ran his hands over her back until he cupped her ass. Then he gave it a playful slap. "Let's leave that for now."

So in this, too, he was going to hold back while she gave everything. Lana fought against the niggling discontent, concentrating instead on the many possible intriguing interpretations she could give that titillating smack on her butt. "I'm not that easily shocked, Brody. I read extensively."

"I bet you do. Pirate romance novels, no doubt."

"Occasionally. But mostly fantasy." At the way his eyes twinkled she smiled. "I was talking about Terry Pratchett, not the kind of fantasy you're thinking of."

Reveling in the freedom to touch him, Lana ran her hands over Brody's shoulders, slipping them down until she could brush her fingers over the flat discs of his nipples. His breath caught and his voice lowered to a seductive octave. "Right now you're talking way too much."

Wriggling, Lana felt the way he hardened against her stomach and surprised pleasure spread through her. "Again?"

"Apparently." He pulled her face to his and gave her a deep, lingering kiss. By the time he drew back Lana was breathless. "You tell me if you get tired, sweetness, because I don't think I'm going to."

"I'll never get tired of this. I *love* sex."

His laugh rippled against her breasts. "I noticed. But I've got twenty that says you'll give in before I do."

Lana planted a kiss against the spot where his heart was

beating, strong and sure beneath her palm. Then she gave his nipple a languid brush with her tongue that made him tangle his fingers convulsively through her hair and arch against her mouth. He seemed to like that as much as she did, which Lana considered powerful ammunition.

She smiled against his skin. "You're on, tough guy."

The shrill ring of the phone jarred Brody from a contented doze. Opening his eyes, it took him a moment to comprehend that afternoon had turned into night. In the next second he became aware of the way Lana's hand was resting against his crotch, lightly cupping his balls like she owned them. She wouldn't be far off if she thought so.

Silence fell again as the phone gave up its quest. Brody smiled as the events of the last few hours played over in his head. The woman was insatiable. The way she'd gone at him that second time had turned sex into a fun kind of competition, a game of who could hold out the longest before coming. Thankfully he'd won that round, albeit by a nose, and the one after that too. But masculine pride was pretty much the only thing giving him an edge and he knew it. The surprises she kept throwing at him, like that fantasy role-play, had caught him off guard and made him want to explode the second he nestled into her tight body.

The damn phone started again and Brody figured it might be important. Reluctantly, he nudged Lana's shoulder. "Hey, sleepyhead. Your phone's ringing."

"Hmmm?" She shifted against his side, the slide of her naked breast against his ribs making his loins stir. He started to swell and Lana noticed. He felt the way her lips curled against his chest a second before she gave him a friendly squeeze.

Brody groaned as he began to turn rigid in her hand. Definitely insatiable. "Your phone's been ringing," he prodded again. "A couple of times."

"Oh. Oh darn, it's probably my mother. She always calls on Monday nights when she knows I'm not working."

She slid out of bed and Brody heard her open her wardrobe door. He leaned over and switched on the lamp, enjoying the view of her naked body in the instant before she covered it with a silky purple robe.

"You owe me twenty." He didn't bother to conceal the erection that hadn't yet diminished as he climbed out of bed and began searching for his shorts.

Lana looked at it and smiled. "Oh I'm not tired. This is merely a time-out."

Brody chuckled to himself as she left the room.

A few minutes later, after using the bathroom and managing to get himself more or less under control, Brody realized he was hungry. Figuring maybe Lana was too—she liked to eat almost as much as she liked to have sex—he headed for the kitchen and started cataloguing ingredients.

She hadn't been kidding about the instant-noodle habit, he thought with a grimace as he found a cupboard full of the Styrofoam bowls. Bypassing them he pulled some bread from the freezer and put it on the counter, then added eggs, milk, dried herbs, a few decrepit-looking zucchini and one lonesome tomato that was about to expire. He tossed the moldy cheese he discovered in her dairy case into the trash.

All the while he listened with half an ear to Lana's side of the phone conversation. It appeared to be largely about bingo, doctor's appointments and Lana's dating schedule. "...no he kept chewing his fingernails at the table... That one totally lied about his age *and* he still lived with his mother... Stop pushing

Tom on me, he's practically my second cousin. Christ, Mum. I know, sorry about the language... No, nobody particular at the moment."

Brody sensed her eyes on him after that last comment, but he kept his focus on whisking the eggs and milk. No reason she should tell her mother about him, especially since they weren't actually *dating* according to Lana's definition. So why should it bother him that she didn't? Because it was one more reminder that he was good enough to fuck but not to date?

He set the bowl down on the counter with a thud, annoyed that he had to remind himself fucking was all he was interested in, as well.

"Sorry about that," she said when she'd ended the call. "She worries I'm turning into a spinster—twenty-three and not even married yet. She likes to make sure I'm at least *trying* to do something about it."

"You don't need help in that department, Lana. You could get married if you wanted to." Lana belonging to somebody else. The notion made it impossible not to chop the overripe tomato without mashing it to a pulp.

"I don't want to get married. *I* think I have plenty of time for that."

"All I'm saying is when you want to, you won't have trouble finding takers." There'd probably be a queue. Especially if any of her potential husbands got a taste of what she was like in bed, of how she could make a man laugh and almost come at the same time. He sliced the end of a zucchini only to discover the inside was brown. Brody sent it the same way as the cheese with a force that almost made the plastic bin topple over.

"You're being very free and easy with my vegetables."

"You call that a vegetable?"

He felt her watching him from the other side of the kitchen.

"Is everything all right?"

"Why wouldn't it be?"

"I don't know. You're acting like you have a vendetta against the contents of my fridge."

"Wasted food makes me crazy." When he was a kid he'd never had enough to spare, but that wasn't the explanation he gave. "Occupational hazard."

"Okay," she said carefully. "What are you making?"

"French toast. You don't have fixings for much else. Really, Lana." He brandished the plastic bottle of generic Italian spice mix. "*Dried* herbs?"

"I like to sprinkle them on my microwave noodles."

He scoffed. "I'm not even going to start on that, or the fact you can make yourself sick eating moldy cheese." He turned to find her grinning at him. "What?"

"You're so cute when you're being a food snob."

"*Cute?* I'm as cute as a pit bull."

She took a few slow steps toward him. The sensuous glide of her walk made his blood rush below his waistband, while his heart did a funny little tumble through his chest. When she reached him she slid her arms around his waist, dropping her forehead onto his shoulder and nuzzling into him, making herself comfortable in a way that constricted his heart. All of a sudden he felt like he couldn't breathe. Jesus, what was wrong with him?

She stood there, holding him—*cuddling* him—because he'd berated the fare available in her pantry, and he was so confounded by all it made him feel he didn't do a damn thing. He thought he should hold her—he *wanted* to hold her, so tight that he'd pull her into him—but his arms wouldn't work. She slid away again, like silk fluttering on the wind, and when she looked at him, her eyes didn't quite connect, not in that lively, direct *Lana* way. Brody felt her absence even though they were separated by a mere two feet.

He'd missed something good, he knew it. An opportunity that might not arise again. But he had no idea how to get it back, or if he should even try. He was still the guy Lana wanted to practice on so she'd be a good lover for someone else. He had no business snuggling with her in the kitchen like they were going to get freaking married.

Suddenly, he didn't feel so hungry anymore. After a moment Lana said, "That was awkward—the phone call. I would have told my mother I had someone over, but I didn't know how to explain this in a way she would find acceptable."

Right now, Brody wasn't sure he could explain it to himself. He sent her a smile. "Hey, the mothers usually prefer not to know about me. I get it."

He regretted hinting at past liaisons when she paled a little. "Are you talking about that girl you stole the peach schnapps for?"

Among others. "Emma was shipped off to boarding school the next day. I think I'm that wrong crowd good girls aren't supposed to mix with. Fair warning, sweetness, hanging around me can be corrupting."

She laughed and the throaty sound of it warmed him, made him relax. "Have you ever thought maybe *I'm* corrupting *you*?"

"Not possible. You're too nice."

"You still think that?" Sidling up to him she slipped her fingers into the waistband of his shorts and tugged him forward until their bodies bumped. He felt the jut of her nipples against his chest through the flimsy robe she wore and his pants billowed like a spinnaker in high knot winds. There was nothing *nice girl* about the way she reached down and cupped his

126

growing erection. "What do I have to do to convince you I'm not so sweet?"

Brody laughed. Never had laughter and desire fused as inextricably as they seemed to with Lana. "Nothing you can do, *sweetness*. You're as decent as they come."

"We'll see." With a skill a woman of her limited experience shouldn't have possessed, she skimmed his fly open and tugged his shorts down until they dropped around his ankles. Taking him in hand, she gave him a long, smooth stroke.

Brody's eyes drifted shut on the pleasure. "You have great hands."

"I think I have a pretty good mouth too," she purred. Then she dropped to her knees and Brody's pulse hammered at the look she sent him from the lowered position. "Will you teach me how to do this?"

Jesus Christ. She flicked out her tongue and ran it along his hard length. Despite already having been to heaven and back three times in the last five hours, Brody could almost have gone there again just from watching her do that. "God, Lana. You don't have to."

"I want to." She opened her smooth, pink lips and wrapped them around him.

Need felt like a burning hunger inside as he sank into her mouth. He was used to women who knew exactly when they were driving a man to breaking point but somehow Lana's timid little sucks, the soft way she stroked him with her hand was more stimulating than the most practiced blow job he'd ever had.

Threading his fingers through the silken mane of her hair, Brody lost himself in the heat of her. He told her what to do, in detail, and got more and more aroused by the eager way she followed each instruction. She did every single thing he asked but Brody wasn't kidding himself. He was at her mercy this time.

It should have embarrassed him how quickly he neared the end. But it was like living a fantasy he'd never even dared dream—that a girl as good, as giving, as Lana, would find him worthy of this. "Lana, stop." He was shocked at how small and breathless his voice sounded.

She lifted her head immediately. "Am I doing something wrong?"

"No." How could she not know everything she did was so right? "I'll come in your mouth if you don't stop."

"Isn't that what you want?"

"You have no idea," he muttered. "But you might not like it."

Her teeth flashed before she lowered her head once more and lapped at his engorged, achy rod. "I guess we'll find out."

She drew him into her mouth in a long wet suck that made his balls tingle and draw up. Holding him still with a hand wrapped around the base, she plunged his dick in and out of her mouth. The little moans of delight she uttered vibrated against his shaft, made it impossible to hold back. His hips surged and the sweet relief spread through his limbs as she swallowed every last drop he released.

His knees gave out on him and he sank to the floor, spent and unsteady. This time he didn't shy away from holding her. Gathering her in his arms, he pulled her into his lap and sighed as she nestled against him. After a moment he sensed the shallowness of her breathing and remarked, "Doing that turned you on."

"Uh-huh."

Could she be any more perfect? He untied the knot holding

her robe together. "Your turn."

"I didn't do it so I'd get something in return."

He knew that, and because of it he wanted to make her come so hard she woke the neighbors. "Do as I say, woman. You're good at it."

"Well, okay." She smiled with obvious relish as she positioned her knees on either side of his hips, moaned long and loud when he took a peaked nipple into his mouth. "I am trying to win that twenty dollars."

Chapter Nine

Lana needed an antidote. Something that would stop her getting hooked on the fantasy she was living.

For a week now, Brody had accepted her open invitation to help broaden her sexual repertoire. Each night, she felt the heat of his gaze on her as the Grill's customers filtered out, sensed the promise inherent in it. She would feel him watching her as they went through the late-night cleaning rituals, the effect of that scrutiny alone enough to make her wet. Her pulse would become threadbare when she thought of what lay ahead as he subtly stalked her with his eyes. She longed for the moment the chores were done and they were alone because she knew he would finally touch her.

And boy, did he touch her.

"Are you making one of those or just communing with the coffee machine?"

Lana turned to see Courtney studying her with a curious gaze, and realized she must have been staring into space again, thinking about Brody and what he did to her. The way he spoke to her, rasped words in the dead of night. *Touch me there... Roll over, put that pillow under your hips... You'll like this position, sweetness... Let me in, beg me for it... I love making you come... I love it when you move like that... I love the way you taste...*

It seemed to Lana that if there was so much about her that

Brody loved, wasn't loving *her* only a step away?

"Ground control to Major Green." Lana jumped at the loud click of Courtney's fingers. "You really are a million miles away. Or has your brain only floated as far as the kitchen?"

Chagrin filled Lana at Courtney's knowing look. At a half an hour before opening, Brody and Mick were hanging out in the restaurant's kitchen, making last-minute preparations while Lana set the tables. That task complete, she'd had the vague idea of fixing herself a caffeine hit before the first lot of customers arrived. That was a bit of a problem of late—most of her thoughts were vague unless they centered on Brody.

"I was going to make a coffee. Do you want one?" Lana asked, avoiding the topic of her wandering mind altogether. Courtney had pretty quickly figured out how far Lana's relationship with Brody had progressed, but thankfully she was happy to keep it a secret. By tacit agreement, she and Brody had made it a point not to let on to the rest of the staff that they were lovers. Brody was the boss and she didn't want his recently acquired habit of bedding the restaurant's head waitress to undermine his position in any way.

"Sure." Courtney stowed her bag in the cupboard behind the bar. "Latte for me."

"Do I smell coffee?" Mick stuck his head around the end of the bar, hopeful expression in place.

"You must have the olfactory sense of a canine."

"I'd love a latte, thanks, Lana." Mick pointedly ignored Courtney's jibe. "And the boss will have a—"

"Double shot black, two sugars," Lana filled in.

"That's the one. Thanks."

A second later he was gone. As Lana operated the espresso machine, Courtney arranged cups on the bar, her hurt almost palpable in the quiet of the empty restaurant. "You need to talk to him," Lana suggested.

"About what? The way our relationship of mutual abuse has disintegrated into cold silence?"

Lana didn't point out that the abuse had always seemed markedly one-sided to her. "Why don't you tell him you like him?"

"Because I don't."

Lana laughed. "Come on, Courtney. It's time to disembark from the Good Ship Denial."

"You should talk about denial. You've got your head stuck so far up in the clouds you've caught altitude sickness."

"I'm not kidding myself about anything," Lana said, but her skin prickled the way it did whenever she tried to tell a lie. She lowered her voice. "I assume you're talking about Brody, but you're wrong. I know what's going on between us."

"So there's not a tiny part of you that's hoping he'll to turn around one day and profess his undying love?"

Her discomfiture intensified and Lana focused firmly on mixing the drinks.

Courtney took her silence for a confession. "Oh, Lana. I'm starting to really worry about you."

"Don't." Courtney's mug made a noticeable thud on the bar when Lana set it down. "Concentrate on your own love life—or *lack thereof.* You're probably jealous because you're too bitter to date a nice guy who really likes you, and I'm getting it from a real man."

Courtney's eyes widened. Lana, too, was shocked at her hitherto untapped capacity for bitchiness. "God, that was awful of me," she gasped. "I'm so sorry, Courtney."

Appearing stung, Courtney concentrated on dumping sugar

in her coffee. "If I'm bitter it's because I've been hurt before. Anyone can see you haven't been, or there's no way you'd throw yourself into this affair with a man who always leaves at the end of the summer. How are you going to feel in a few months when he takes off again—assuming this fling of yours even lasts that long?"

It was something Lana had steadfastly refused to think about. *The Good Ship Denial.* Was Courtney right?

No. She wasn't in denial, she was simply determined. She saw the end result she wanted and she was working toward it. Negativity wouldn't get her anywhere.

"I'll be fine, no matter what happens," Lana said. "I'd never expect him to stick around here just for me." Besides, she wasn't averse to going with him next time he sailed off into the sunset. There was nothing she'd like better than to have that man all to herself on the wide blue ocean.

It was possible he'd want her to join him. Wasn't it?

"I still don't think you know what you're getting into."

Lana grew more exasperated with Courtney's pessimism. "That's my problem, not yours."

"I was only trying to be a friend. Something tells me you're going to need one."

Courtney whirled around and collided with Mick, who was striding into the bar like a man on a mission. The impact jostled the mug Courtney carried, causing the hot contents to spill down her arm. Mick looked so distraught that Lana simply moved out of the way as he shepherded Courtney toward the sink and ran her hand under cold water.

Courtney tried to shake off his assistance but Mick continued to fuss, an air of grim determination surfacing. He really cared about her, Lana realized, and a pang of envy gripped her chest. She wished for a moment that she had been attracted to Mick, instead of Brody. Being in love with someone like Mick would be so much easier.

Don't be stupid, Lana. You just told Courtney she was jealous of you. All the sanctimonious certainty of a minute ago seeped out of her as Mick spoke, his voice soft and firm at the same time. "Have a drink with me, Court."

Courtney's voice trembled. "Why would you want to?"

"Haven't you figured that out yet? Because I like you, dummy."

Feeling like an intruder, Lana took the remaining drinks and slipped quietly out to the kitchen, where she caught Brody peering through the service station. When he saw her he jumped back guiltily. "That mine?" He indicated the mug in her hand.

"Yep." Lana slid it down on the counter in front of him. "Were you spying on Courtney and Mick?"

He scoffed. "Why would I do that?"

Lana recalled the way Mick had come firing into the bar, a man full of purpose and bravado. "You told him to ask her out."

"It's about time those two got it together," he grumbled. "Mick's been useless in here."

"Ah. So you did it for the restaurant then."

"Why else?"

Lana hid her smile in her flat white. Brody was actually matchmaking. Her heart did a little dance. Deep down, he was a big softie. If he cared this much about Mick's love life, it stood to reason one day soon he'd start giving a damn about his own.

He sipped his coffee. "This is good. Exactly the way I like it."

Lana smiled and let him think about all the other things she was learning to do precisely the way he wanted. His gaze followed the curl of her lips, a flash of amber lighting the depths of his eyes. She'd give anything to be free to kiss him, but theirs wasn't that kind of relationship.

Is it a relationship at all, Lana? Midnight sex and nothing else?

"You're closing up again tonight?" His voice rumbled with soft intent.

Lana pushed aside the pesky concern that Brody never seemed to want to spend the day with her, or even the morning. He was always gone by dawn, usually before she awoke. Each stealthy departure stung a little, as had the times he'd turned away from the few affectionate gestures she'd tried to make, and every time he avoided talking about himself when she'd encouraged him to.

Yet he wanted her, still, after a week. She hadn't been confident of making it this far, so anything could happen yet. Demanding too much too soon would be a serious tactical error. "Courtney was supposed to close but I think she might want to leave early tonight, so I'll do it."

"I should probably follow you home. I don't trust that Pee Wee contraption you call transport."

"It's called a Bee Wee, and as I've told you many times, it's very reliable."

He eyed her over the rim of his mug. "I'll feel better if I see you get home safe."

Lana held his gaze. "And who'll protect me from you?"

"No one." His focus drifted indolently over her body. "You'll be wide open."

Probably ten seconds after she stepped into her flat, Lana thought, her blood igniting. She tried not to sound as breathless as she felt. "Oh, no. What on earth will happen to me?"

It was as though the air between them was filled with possibilities, with memories. So many times he'd taken things slow and snippets of recollection flashed through Lana's mind. Each panted breath, the way he made her body stretch and give, every cry for mercy that tore from her throat, the countless explosions of pleasure that seemed to extend into forever.

From the fire in his eyes, Lana knew tonight would not be one of those times. He'd be all over her the second they were alone. Perhaps they wouldn't make it to the bed, like a few nights ago, when he'd bent her forward over the back of the couch and spread her open, ramming inside—

"Five minutes 'til opening," Mick announced jauntily as he bounded into the kitchen. "Then it's all happening."

It would be much closer to five hours before anything *really* interesting happened. Now heavily aroused, Lana wondered how she was going to wait that long. Tamping down the wild anticipation, she turned to Mick and hoped her flushed complexion wasn't too obvious. "I take it things went well with Courtney?"

"She's agreed to a date. All thanks to this guy." He indicated Brody with a huge grin. "He told me to get my shit together and take charge of the situation, and now I have a date with an angel."

"Get your shit together and take charge," Lana repeated, glancing at Brody. "This is what you call wisdom?"

"Women like a man who can steer the ship." Brody flashed her a grin. Cheeky, friendly, but devoid of the heat that had pulsed between them a moment ago. The shutters had come down the second Mick had walked in. He was always so much better at retreating than she was.

Lana wrestled with the flutter of panic that realization

provoked, trying to match Brody's teasing but detached tone. "I'll have to inform all women everywhere that Brody Nash knows what women want. Perhaps I'll take out an ad in the paper."

"Make it a billboard," Mick suggested. "And don't forget to mention that Courtney Fitzsimmons finally admitted she has a thing for me."

The restaurant was busy and it was almost midnight by the time Lana parked her scooter under her carport. Brody was right behind her, and she hadn't even fitted her key into the door when she felt his hands on her shoulders, drawing her against him, turning her around, kissing the breath from her lungs. Her front door was sheltered by an alcove, and Brody took her into the shadows, nestling her against the cool stucco wall. He palmed her breasts. She wound her legs around him. Moments later her panties were pushed aside and he was there, sheathed and ready, as though he'd been ready since that flirting heat in the kitchen, like she had been. He said, "Slow once we get inside. Fast now," and entered her with a conquering thrust.

The street outside her duplex was dark, but the forbidden thrill of being in the open made her crazy for him. Lana gripped him tight, whispered, "Yes. Fuck me right here. I love when you take me rough with your hard cock."

"*Jesus.*" He rocked into her, stunned into an increased pace by her words. She'd wanted to use them, to shake off the innate conservatism of her upbringing and embrace the wildness he brought out in her, and now she relished the way her boldness turned him impatient and quietly desperate in the shadows. His cheek rasped against hers, his breath coming fast against her hair. Pushing up her blouse he touched her breasts and she curved into him, offering herself like a sacrifice as he pounded into her and, for the first time since the night of Drew

137

and Sidney's wedding, released himself into rapture before he took her there.

Lana didn't care about that—she knew he'd make up for it once they were inside. The strength of his need for her was a better knowledge. *He needed her.* It didn't matter that he never voiced it quite like that, or that he could act remote when he chose to. When they were alone, he needed her, at least physically. The rest would come in baby steps.

Perhaps all he needed was a little more encouragement.

Chapter Ten

"Hey there, mate. Hard at work I see."

Brody turned to see Drew standing in the doorway of the Grill's kitchen, tanned and relaxed in shorts and a surf shirt. He looked like a man who'd just spent the better part of two weeks swimming and screwing around with his new wife. Something sparked like a lit match inside Brody and with a shock he realized it was jealousy.

He'd felt it before, used to feel it all the time when he saw Drew and Sidney together. He'd thought he was green because he was in love with Sidney. Now with the benefit of hindsight he could see it had never been about that. He envied what they had, the way they were together. A couple of puzzle pieces that fit perfectly.

Why in hell should he be envious that Drew had something he didn't want anyway?

"Back already?" Speech proved difficult when confusion swirled around in Brody's mind. "Give us a chance to miss you why don't you?"

"Are you saying you're doing better on your own?"

"I wouldn't want to hurt your feelings by confirming it."

"Since when have you been concerned with anyone's feelings?"

It was only their usual trash talk, the nature of his and Drew's relationship, but for some reason the comment stung. "Maybe I've changed." Why had he said that?

Drew's brows hiked but thankfully his friend didn't investigate the meaning of his out-of-character comment. Instead he glanced around the kitchen, at the foodstuffs littering the counters. "You're cleaning out the cool room? Jeez, Brody, you should have made one of the apprentices do that. You bored or something?"

Bored? Far from it. Too damn interested, more like it. He had to work hard to fill the empty hours in his day before the restaurant opened. If he sat around on the boat, his mind invariably strayed to Lana. He'd wonder what she was doing, how she spent her time without him. If she was always tinkering on her computer or if she had other interests he didn't know about.

Occasionally anxiety would set in. He'd picture her seeing some other guy during the day. She'd never promised they'd be exclusive and he wasn't about to ask her to. Because he didn't want that either, he always told himself, ignoring the fact he hadn't even looked at another woman since his first night back in town. Not because the thought of another man putting his hands on Lana made him want to break heads.

And not because he thought he and Lana could have what Drew and Sidney had. At least he knew *he* couldn't have that. Long ago he'd decided not to even ask for it, because he'd had enough disillusionment in his life, and he was smart enough not to invite more. There was something to be said for not aiming too high.

He had to keep things with Lana on a purely sexual basis, which meant no daytime visits, no reading the paper over morning coffee. No mixed messages, like she'd asked from the beginning.

"Not bored—sucking up to the boss," Brody finally responded to Drew's question. "Heard he was coming back from his honeymoon today and thought he might want to give me tomorrow off."

"You taking the boat out?"

Brody shrugged. He hadn't specifically planned to, hadn't felt that need to get the hell away from everyone like he usually did. But he often went for a sail on his days off if the weather conditions were favorable, and it would put some distance between him and Lana, which had to be a smart thing when he had a whole day of temptation to fight. "Maybe."

"Fair enough. I'll come in tonight and you can give me the rundown on the last two weeks."

"You promised me one more night before we went back to being slaves to the restaurant." The words were punctuated by a loud slap as Sidney Buchanan strode into the room and soundly whacked her husband on the seat of his pants. "What's this about working tonight?"

"Only for an hour or two, I promise."

"Sure, sure," Sidney muttered doubtfully. "Don't expect me to follow suit. I'll be at home." She smiled suggestively. "Waiting."

The look Drew gave his new wife was decidedly ravenous. He told Brody, "On second thought, perhaps you can deal on your own for one more night."

"Ack." Brody pretended disgust. "Didn't you two get enough of each other on the honeymoon?"

Sidney turned and grinned sassily at him. "You'd think so, wouldn't you? Mauritius was glorious. I'd show you the photos but they might make you blush."

Brody smirked. "I'm not the blushing type, Sid."

"Don't I know it." She walked over and punched him playfully on the arm, following up with a kiss on the cheek that he responded to with a bear hug that for once felt entirely natural. When he'd come back to town, Brody had been a little afraid that the sexual buzz might still exist between them, but now when he hugged her it was an utterly platonic thing. He did love Sidney, but he didn't want her in that way anymore.

Eventually, Sidney laughed and pulled back. "It's good to have you back at the restaurant. We miss you when you go."

"It's nice to be needed." He'd meant it as a joke but something in the words rang true. This time when he'd returned to Graceville, it wasn't only a product of his own necessity, but because Drew had asked him to take over the restaurant. Brody realized he felt glad he'd been able to do that for his friend, and running the Grill hadn't been nearly as burdensome as he'd thought it might be. He hadn't pissed anyone off so much they'd quit, and he'd kind of liked the sense of accomplishment he'd gotten from being in charge.

A loud crash made them all turn toward the door of the kitchen, where a tray of wine glasses lay shattered on the floor. Brody's pulse gave a sharp thump when his gaze collided with Lana's. Her eyes shot from his face to the place where his arm was still draped around Sidney's shoulders. Something glittered hard in her golden irises before she dropped to her haunches and began collecting the broken glassware.

Jealousy. Brody recognized its white-hot flare because it was the same thing he felt whenever Mick Jensen said something to make Lana giggle or tugged on her ponytail in a mischievous manner. It didn't make sense because he'd long figured out that Lana had no interest in the other chef, and Mick's infatuation with Courtney was obvious. Lana didn't let

Mick take her home and fuck her senseless, so Brody had no reason to feel homicidal every time he saw the two of them together, but he did anyway.

Lana gasped and swore, bringing her finger to her mouth and sucking it. Realizing that she'd cut herself, Brody rushed toward her, shaking off the disturbing understanding that despite all his efforts, at some stage he and Lana had pushed things past casual sex and into emotional territory. The thought gathered weight when he grabbed her hand and saw the slice on her index finger. The sight of her blood increased the tightness in his chest, which engaged his temper. "What the hell were you doing, Lana? You could have seriously hurt yourself."

"It's only a little cut."

She tried to draw her hand away but he couldn't bring himself to release it. "We've got band-aids in the first aid cabinet. Sid..."

"Here, I've got them." Sidney handed him the box she'd already grabbed, nodding at Lana. "Hi, Lana."

Lana's lips formed a smile that encompassed both Sidney and Drew. Brody could tell it was forced because her eyes were devoid of the impish sparkle that lit them when she flat-out grinned in her usual, open way. The way she grinned at him. "Welcome back. How was the trip?"

"Fabulous."

While Sidney gave her a brief rundown on the hotel they'd stayed in, Brody applied a band-aid to Lana's wound. "This cut's deep. You should have been more careful."

Lana protested in a snippy voice. "I'm fine. I don't need you to treat me like a kid."

Brody bit down on a laugh. He hadn't been treating her like a kid lately and she damn well knew it. "What are you doing here anyway? Your shift doesn't start for hours."

He met her eyes and saw they'd narrowed to angry slits. "I was passing and thought I'd pick up my pay slip."

Bullshit. She could have done that tonight. Had she engineered the excuse in order to see him? It was exactly the kind of thing he'd schooled himself not to do since they'd started this thing. Brody was surprised Lana had been the one to break first. Didn't she know better? She had to keep guys like him at arm's length.

Didn't *he* know better than to get a kick out of the fact she hadn't been able to?

"Your slip's behind the bar with all the others," Brody said, jerking his head in that direction. He forced himself to drop her hand with effort. Like he didn't want to let her go. *Fuck.*

"Great. I'll get it and leave. I can see how busy you are."

She hesitated. Brody crossed his arms over his chest to stop himself touching her. From hauling her into his arms and telling her not to go, to stay here and chuck out the bruised tomatoes with him. With her that'd be fun.

What was *wrong* with him?

"I guess I'll see you tonight then." He sounded rude but he didn't care. He was so damned mad at her. She couldn't afford to get attached to him like this, because he was not going to get attached back. Now there was a very real possibility he was going to hurt her feelings and he'd never wanted to do that.

"Peachy," she said pithily. "Can't wait."

Like a whirlwind she was gone again, leaving Brody feeling pissed and bereft, even more pissed because of the bereft thing, and semi-hard inside his jockey shorts. This was not good. Not good at all.

He turned to see two pairs of eyes watching him with

suspicion. "What?"

Sidney shook her head, disillusionment in the action. "Oh, Brody."

"*What?*"

"She's talking about my best waitress, shithead." Drew sounded resigned. As though despite the little talk they'd had, he hadn't expected any better. "Did you have to?"

The blood drained from his face. *They knew.* Three and a half minutes in the same room with him and Lana, and they knew. Had the rest of the staff figured it out? Had they been snickering behind their backs? Brody couldn't give a toss what they thought of him, but Lana didn't deserve to be treated like a bawdy joke. If he found out any of the guys had been talking about her like that, he'd thump the living snot out of them.

He struggled through his fury to find the only two people whose opinions mattered still staring at him warily. His skin felt downright itchy. *Shame,* he realized. He should have known Lana wasn't the kind of girl who could stay uninvolved, despite all she'd said to the contrary. He felt bloody ashamed of himself for taking his own pleasure at her expense. "It's all right," he said even as he wondered if it was true. "I'm not going to hurt her."

"Oh, Brody," Sidney said again, in that knowing way that made him feel like he was missing some vital piece of information. "Don't you know how she feels about you?"

His heart started hammering. "I can see she's read more into the situation than she should have."

"I'm not talking about that. She's had feelings for you for a long time. I can't believe you didn't know it."

Brody scowled. "Nah. We hooked up at the wedding. It's your fault." Brody pointed a finger at Drew. "You had to go and get married. You know how women are about weddings." They started feeling all romantic and wistful, which turned into horny and before a guy knew it he found a girl waiting for him in his bed.

"Don't blame my getting married for your stupidity. Ever heard that old rule 'don't shit where you eat'?"

"You know I don't give a hang about rules." He paced the kitchen. "Where the hell were you when I needed you? You're the one who stops me from going off the rails."

"I was a tad distracted with getting married."

"What were you thinking leaving me in charge here? I don't do well with responsibility, you know that."

"So sorry, but I was in Mauritius on my *fucking honeymoon.*"

"Guys, simmer down." Sidney's command made both their mouths clam shut. She glared at Brody from her low-down five-foot-four-inch perch, and the look she gave him made Brody shake with what felt suspiciously like fear. "You're going to break her heart."

Her quiet statement sent the shakes outward. Brody ran a hand through his hair. His fingers trembled. "No." He denied it hotly. "She's too smart for that."

"Brody, no one's too smart for that."

"What is everyone getting so worked up about?" Brody threw up his hands. "This hasn't gone so far it can't be reversed. I'm going to fix this."

"What, by dumping her?" Drew asked.

"God no." Look into those eyes and tell her it was nice while it lasted but it was getting to be a big yawn? He might as well put on a hockey mask and go scream at some children, it couldn't make him feel any more like a monster. "I told you, she's smart. She knows what a bad prospect I am, that this isn't going anywhere. I'll help her remember it. She'll dump me."

Sidney and Drew shared a look, some silent communication passing between them. A moment later Sidney shook her head at Brody, muttered a goodbye and disappeared out the door.

Drew turned back to Brody and asked, "Is that really what you want? For Lana to end things with you?"

No way. It had been little more than a week of fun, satisfying, lusty sex, the best sex of his life. He hadn't had nearly enough of it. But what he wanted wasn't necessarily what was best for Lana. He couldn't lead her on and hurt her any more than he may already have done. "It's the way it has to be. She deserves better."

"That sounds like your father's bullshit talking."

Brody's blood chilled. He had an abrupt, violent urge to take a swing at his best friend, hit him so hard he dropped. While Mrs. Buchanan might pry a little at times, without having to be asked Drew had always left the topic of Brody's parents well and truly alone.

Silence breathed between them like an evil spirit stirring up trouble. At length Brody spoke, his voice sounding as cold and hard as the stainless steel surrounding them. "You know squat about that."

"You think I didn't overhear him sometimes when I came up the walk, before he shut up because he realized I was there? I heard the things he used to say to you." Drew shook his head, a faraway look in his eyes. "The fact that he used to smack you around when he was drunk was almost incidental. The way he screwed with your head was what really messed you up. He used to say you were stupid and worthless. He told you your mother left because of you."

"She did leave because of me."

"She left because your dad was an asshole."

"Then why didn't she take me with her?" Was that his voice breaking? *Shit.* His stomach roiled at the memories. A strange guy in a red car, his mother in a blue dress, carrying a suitcase. Her anguished tears when he'd begged her to stay. *I can't handle it, Brody. I'm so sorry, but I never wanted to be a mother.*

"I don't want to talk about this," he said slowly, carefully. "It has nothing to do with what's going on now."

"It has everything to do with it," Drew refuted. "People won't necessarily leave if you let yourself love them. I saw the way you and Lana were looking at each other. No way she wants to dump you, and I don't think you want her to either."

"What I want isn't relevant, and she will dump me." He'd been too agreeable of late, that was the problem. Getting repeatedly laid by a beautiful girl had a way of improving a man's mood. Once Lana remembered what he was really like, she'd see sense and kick him to the curb. It was the ideal solution.

Drew sighed, sounding defeated. Brody turned and started packing up the empty boxes ready for the recycling bin. Drew's footsteps retreated, then stopped at the door. "Listen, I'm going to say something you'll probably never let me live down, but I have to say it. I love you, man. Even that stuff with Sidney last April, I didn't hate you for that. It scared the shit out of me, thinking I could lose her to you, not just because it would have meant I couldn't have her, but because things between us would never have been the same. I don't know if I could have still been your friend if you'd taken her from me, and I think I would have missed you almost as much as Sid."

Brody's hands stilled on the boxes but he didn't turn around. "She was never going to leave you, Drew. She didn't love me."

"Yeah, but you know what terrified me? I think a part of her wanted to. Women always want to love you, Brody," Drew told him. "You just don't let them."

Lana figured she had two choices. She could lie down and play dead, or she could go for broke.

Right away, she'd realized the mistake she'd made by going to the restaurant. When she'd walked in on Brody hugging a petite blonde, she'd seen so much red it was like the sun had gone supernova. By the time she realized the woman was Sidney and the hug was only a friendly one, she'd already broken the glasses and they were all staring at her. Right at the truth she couldn't hide.

Brody most keenly of all. He'd worked out she had formed an attachment, that she'd violated the rules of their steamy-sex-but-no-emotions agreement. She'd never been surer of anything in this life.

He planned to end it with her.

And he wasn't even going to be nice about it.

All night he'd found excuse after excuse to criticize her work. Either she took too long to take out the meals or she hadn't written down the orders legibly enough. He'd never had a complaint about her handwriting before so she knew he was doing it to tick her off. And boy, was it working.

"Wake up, Lana," he snapped after one occasion on which she'd had to take a meal back to the kitchen to be amended. "If they ask for baked potato, don't write down mashed, all right?"

"They changed their mind," she said through gritted teeth. At least she thought they had. It was hard to know what was going on when her brain was preoccupied with Brody's nasty mood.

"Are you sure you didn't get distracted?" he sneered. "You seem a little off with the fairies tonight. Try and keep your mind on the job."

Like it wasn't his fault she was distracted? Lana replied with a venomous curl of her lips. "It seems to *me* you've brought your mulish-ass personality to work tonight. Maybe you ought to shut up and do *your* job."

Beside her, Courtney gasped. Behind Brody, Mick let out a snort of laughter. Brody whirled around and glowered at him. "What's so funny, Jensen?"

Mick held up his hands. "Nothing, Chef. Nothing at all."

Once Mick had scuttled off to a faraway corner of the kitchen, Brody turned around again. He caught Lana watching him, and she could swear she saw something other than cold anger in his eyes. For an instant he looked acutely unhappy.

Then his dark gaze went as hard as slate again. "What are you still doing standing there? People are waiting. Chop, chop."

Chop, chop? Oh how she'd love to chop him off at the knees!

Lana stomped through the rest of her shift, asking to be the first to go home when lately she'd insisted on staying until closing so she would be left alone with Brody. She peeled her scooter out of the parking lot with a vigor that would have gotten a Harley rider's attention and spent half the night tossing and turning in her empty bed, fuming at Brody because for the first time in over a week he wasn't under the covers with her. And what was worse, she didn't even *want* him to be.

Gasping, Lana shot up in bed. "That's it!" Her exclamation echoed off the walls. He was intentionally making her furious because he knew if he did, she wouldn't want to share her bed with him. She should have known. He didn't like to take responsibility for anyone else. He wasn't trying to end it with her.

He was trying to get her to end it with him.

"That sneaky jerk." Knowing she wouldn't sleep, Lana got out of bed and made herself a cup of tea. Brody wanted her to end it with him. So why didn't he say their affair had run its course and it was time to finish it? Was he really that incapable of having a meaningful conversation or was there more to it?

What if he didn't *want* things to be over? What if he couldn't bring himself to break it off because he wasn't quite ready to give her up? What if he couldn't bring himself to hurt her like that? That must mean he cared about her, at least a little. Mustn't it?

Lana realized there was only one way to get the answers she sought. She could deal with this situation one of two ways. Accept it and take it lying down like a wimp. Or stand up and face it like a woman.

So what was she—a woman or a wimp?

By three a.m. Lana had her answer. Throwing on a pair of jeans, she stormed out of her apartment and headed for her scooter.

Chapter Eleven

"Hey!"

Brody woke with a start to find Lana standing over him. For a second he was disorientated. He thought he was back in her apartment and wondered how he'd gotten there. He'd made a concerted effort not to give in to the needy urge to seek her out, to tell her how sorry he was. He couldn't start apologizing for who he was or he'd run out of breath.

Sitting up, he realized he was on the *Sunset* and he had a massive headache. The half-empty bottle of rum on the table in front of him explained the second. What he didn't get was Lana's reason for being here. Was she a sucker for punishment? "What time is it?"

"It's three fifteen and well past time we sorted a few things out."

Surveying her face, Brody couldn't help but appreciate how sexy she looked when she was steamed. Her amber eyes snapped like the lick of flames on wood. Her hair fanned wildly around her flushed cheeks. She was breathing heavily, and his gaze dropped inexorably to the rapid rise and fall of her chest through the white tank top she wore. Without a bra.

Brody swallowed and forced his attention back to her face. It was no better. Everywhere he looked she was so beautiful it hurt to see her. He stood and presented her with his back.

"There's nothing to sort out. Go home."

"So you can drink yourself into oblivion?" The remains of rum sloshed as she lifted the bottle. "Is this how you deal with things you don't want to face?"

The question stung like a hard slap, the kind his father used to dish out after he'd spent an afternoon imbibing to chase the blues away. Larry's poison of choice had been scotch, but the cowardly decision to avoid, to not face things head-on, was the same. Jesus, if he was that much like his father he really didn't want Lana anywhere near him.

"I'm not going to make it so easy," she announced. "If I'm going to go through this the hard way, so are you."

"What the hell are you talking about?" Brody swung around. "What this?"

"Us."

"There is no us. What do you think I've been trying to tell you? It's run its course, babe." What a lie that was. Even angry at her for pushing him, he was still drawn to her. In fact the gutsy move she'd made in coming here had admiration swelling in his chest, even while it reinforced all the reasons he had to let her go. She was a much better person than he was, for a start.

She narrowed her eyes at him. "Is that so?"

"It's a damn shame you can't take a hint or I wouldn't have to be so blunt."

She laughed bitterly. "Is that what you call what happened tonight—a hint? I've got news for you, Brody, you don't know how to do subtle. And who says you get to decide when we've run the course?"

"I do. You're twenty-three and you don't know what you're doing."

"You're twenty-eight and you don't have a clue either."

He frowned, hating that she had a valid point. How was he supposed to argue against valid points? She was a woman, she could talk rings around him and they both knew it. He couldn't possibly debate her on any rational level or he'd lose and they'd end up in bed.

Since when was finding yourself in bed with a woman you can't get enough of losing?

Brody grappled for something to fight her with. "I'm the guy," he finally said. Chauvinism. They always hated chauvinism. "I make the moves, I get to end it."

To his surprise she didn't rise to the bait as he'd expected. Instead she threw back her head and laughed. He wondered if she was realizing, as he was, that none of the moves in this affair had ever felt like his.

When she was done making fun of him, she regarded him thoughtfully. "You really are desperate to get rid of me. Why is that?"

When had she taken a step closer? Before he knew it she was standing before him, challenging him with those incredible eyes. He could smell her. No perfume, just plain soap and a smile, with the added headiness of something else. Determination and arousal. The tightness in his pants got worse.

"Do you really not want me anymore? Because I have to say it was a very fast about-face. As recently as last night you seemed to want me fine. Three times in fact. Remember that?"

How could he forget? Every single moment he'd spent inside her body was indelibly etched on his memory. But he was powerless to stop her as she painted him the picture. "I woke up and you were right there behind me, so close we felt like one person. You were so hard and I was so wet, it was the

154

most natural thing in the world for you to slide inside me." She settled in close to his chest, pressing her breasts to him as she trailed a fingernail down his face. Everything he was throbbed at her closeness. His cock ached to be inside her—her mouth, her pussy. He didn't care, just as long as it was *her*.

It scared the shit out of him.

Arousal swamped the fear and washed it away as she continued. "Then you fucked me, didn't you, Brody? You fucked me like a man who didn't want to stop. And when you came you said, 'I can't get enough of you, sweetness.' Are you trying to tell me you were lying?"

No, he hadn't lied. He never wanted to lie to her. That's why he figured it was better to keep conversation to a minimum, their relationship strictly sexual. But what happened today made him realize that he'd failed in that endeavor. She was starting to want more, things he couldn't give.

Placing his hands on her hips he tried to move her away from him. But when his fingers grazed flesh just above the low-riding waistband of her jeans, need took over. He pulled her to him instead, grinding her against the rigid swelling in his pants. "You should go, Lana."

She smiled and he knew how plainly his words contradicted his actions. "I don't want to. The way I see it, we can handle things one of two ways. You stomp around being rude and keep pushing and pushing until I have no option but to give up on you to save myself. As much as I want you, I won't put up with being treated like dirt every other week because you can't handle what's going on between us."

Didn't she see that was exactly what he was trying to save her from?

In a sinuous motion, she twined her arms around his neck and pressed her soft length more tightly to his body. He could feel the sharp impression of her nipples bumping his chest and dizziness made the cabin spin. He wasn't fully drunk, but inebriated enough that his defenses were far too weak to withstand this kind of assault.

Or perhaps that had nothing to do with alcohol. His defenses always seemed pervious when it came to Lana.

"The second option—and I like this one much better—is we don't end this because you've arbitrarily decided it's time. We want each other." She demonstrated her point by wriggling her hips against his, letting him know his fierce erection hadn't gone unnoticed. "We're both adults. Why don't we continue to do what comes naturally? When you can look me in the eye and tell me like you mean it that you don't want me in your bed, I'll walk away. Until then..."

She let the promise hang in the air as she pressed her lips to his throat, swirling her tongue around the pulse point. Brody groaned and bunched his hands in the flesh of her backside, rubbing the denim covering her crotch against his hard-on. She lifted her legs and wrapped them around his hips, locking on and matching his motions with unveiled enthusiasm. He loved the way she always responded with such candid passion, how she never tried to hide anything from him. He respected her for it, even as her honesty made his own omissions seem like subterfuge.

No, he had never out and out lied to her. But there were things he refused to tell, places he wouldn't let her go because they made him feel ashamed, worthless. He didn't want to tell her all that stuff about his mum and dad. He'd never told anyone, and that had never mattered before. But with Lana he was tempted to share and his inability to do so had begun to gather significance.

Her lips made their way around to his. She breathed

panting breaths against his mouth. "I want everything tonight, Brody. I want you to do all the things you don't do because you think they'll scare me. And then I want you inside me, big and hard and hot, fucking me, making me scream for more."

Her words fired his blood. His dick felt pained where she rubbed herself against it. He couldn't believe she was saying these things, his sweet Lana. The woman who'd stormed in here all fired up when she should have been doing the four-minute mile in the opposite direction surprised him. Surprised him and turned him on like nobody's business. This woman wouldn't shrink away from his need to control, to mark, to dominate. She'd give as good as she got and be ready to go another round before the night was over.

But still he hesitated. If he stepped over that threshold, good or bad, he sensed nothing would be the same again. "Lana, look at me."

She drew back and met his gaze. *No fear.* She was tenacious and beautiful, and he couldn't believe she'd go to all this trouble for him. He'd meant to give her one last chance to change her mind, but he could see from her expression that nothing would make her do that. Instead he touched her face and said words he meant with every fiber of his being. "I'm sorry for the way I spoke to you tonight. I will never treat you like that again."

Her eyes glistened. "I won't let you get away with it."

He carried her to the cabin and laid her on the bed, cupping her breasts through the fabric of her top. There was a little moonlight drifting in through the porthole but he wanted more, wanted to see her. He switched on his reading lamp, grabbing a condom from his stash while he was there. When he turned back and saw her lying there, her arms and legs spread out like she was offering herself to him, his knees buckled. He didn't deserve her.

She made a breathy request that stripped him of any vestige of nobility. "My shirt...rip it off."

Swearing softly, he fell to his knees on the mattress, bracketing her hips. He found the hem of her top and fisted it. A shredding sound rent the air as he ripped the material, exposing her breasts. Lust fired in her eyes, lighting a match to his own desire and turning it to a conflagration. Falling on her, he feasted on her flesh, drawing first one, then the other swollen crest into his mouth. He sucked her hard and Lana threw herself against him with abandon, her body a beautiful curve in the low light.

Grasping at her jeans and panties, he pulled them over her hips, revealing her glistening thatch. When she tried to kick the denims off he stopped her. "No. Like that." The material was wrapped around her ankles, preventing her legs from spreading wide as she obviously wanted them to. He ran his finger along the seam of her lips, avoiding her clit, and watched as she writhed in helpless need. "What do you want me to do? Tell me."

There was no shyness or hesitation. "Touch my clit. Rub it until I come."

"Jesus you're beautiful. Beautiful and dirty." He smiled and gave her labia a little squeeze that teased the sensitive nerve endings that wanted his hand, his tongue to bring release. He denied her that, for now. "Roll onto your stomach."

She groaned in disappointment but did as he bid without question. It was apparent she liked it when he took control, was eager to play the role of his little love slave. The knowledge made his cock expand and harden so painfully he had to strip off his pants. Being naked helped ease the irritation.

That was until Lana wriggled her hips on the bed, causing

her tight ass to undulate sensuously. As he watched she slipped her hand beneath her stomach, seeking out her excited flesh. Brody enjoyed the view and let her toy with herself until he sensed her approaching a point of no return. Grabbing her wrist, he pinned it to the mattress above her head. "I'm going to let you come soon, sweetness. Not yet."

He released her hand so he could use both of his to caress her shoulders. He ran his touch along her spine until he encountered the swell of her glutes. She had such tight buns, and she was so taut and narrow inside that he was tempted to sink into her right now, fuck her from behind with her laid out flat on his bed. The need burned him and he closed his eyes to stop the urge. He wanted more, and she wanted to know how much more there was. The thought of showing her called to him more loudly than the need for immediate gratification.

"Get up on your knees. Not on all fours," he said when she made to do that. "Keep your hands flat on the bed and point that ass nice and high in the air for me. I want to see it when I mark it."

Lana's heart pounded as she followed Brody's instructions. Oh God, he was going to leave his imprint on her there, spank her. She'd been fantasizing about it ever since that night he hadn't divulged his fantasies but she'd sensed them anyway. Now it was really going to happen and she was so wet her thighs slipped together as she moved. She suspected she'd be able to orgasm from merely squeezing her legs together.

When she tried to, he laughed softly. "Don't do that. Spread 'em apart for me. Show me that pretty little pussy of yours."

Groaning, she moved her knees on the bed, parting them as far as they could go with her jeans around her ankles. He sighed, a sound of appreciation. "That's so nice. You have no idea." Dipping a finger into her channel, he pumped it a couple of times, tickling her inner walls before withdrawing. She heard him suckle the juice off his finger and cried in protest. He'd done that before and she always wished he'd licked the cream directly out of her. He knew that, the tease.

"Stay right there." She heard his footsteps retreating into the saloon.

Lana kept her arms flat out on the mattress as he'd told her to. The position made her feel exposed and vulnerable, but so horny she began to worry over how long she'd last before she came. She didn't want this to end too soon.

There was a soft plop as something hit the mattress beside her head. Lana turned to see a coil of rope. "Do you remember that night I strapped you to your bed, Lana?"

How could she forget? "I remember."

Dipping his head, he whispered in her ear. "Remember how much you liked it when I made you submit, made you say you loved what I was doing to you?"

"Yes."

The bed shifted as Brody climbed on it, his knees planted on the mattress beside her. He began threading the rope around her wrists. "I'm going to make you beg again tonight, Lana. I'm going to put you over my knee and spank your sexy little ass."

With a deft tug he secured her wrists together with the rope so her hands were bound in front of her. Then he moved to her feet, got rid of her jeans and proceeded to bind her ankles too. She tried to wriggle free but the rope was tight, yet not so tight it cut off her circulation. She had suspected Brody might want to do this, and she wasn't shocked or afraid. "I know. I've been thinking about it."

"You have?"

She nodded, her cheek rasping against the sheets.

"Look at me."

Lifting her head Lana saw the surprise in his eyes, the heat. She smiled, enjoying that she could shock him, could make him want her so badly his irises glowed, revealing the hidden amber flecks in them. He ran his hands over her body peremptorily, as if she had little right or ability to stop him. He gave her backside a rough squeeze. "You've been fantasizing about me punishing you?"

Lana rasped, "Yes."

"What were your fantasies like?"

He slapped her on the cheek, lightly. He barely touched her really. But the contact made Lana gasp. "Like this. Exactly like this. Except..."

"Except?"

Her heart throbbed with her admission, pounding against her chest. "You used a belt on me too."

Muttering an oath, he swooped down and captured her mouth in a hot, rough kiss. His touch seared over her, leaving a trail of fire behind until he found her breasts and squeezed them. Lana moaned against his mouth and writhed into his touch, wanting more of his forceful passion, needing him to be out of control even while she knew he mastered her with absolute power.

When he pulled back he was breathing hard. Lana was so dizzy she thought she might pass out. "And to think I thought you were a good girl."

"First impressions aren't always right."

"That's what I'm discovering. You're definitely not too nice to be put over my knee."

Brody moved her until her elbows rested on the mattress

on one side of his bent legs, her knees on the other. The position made the tips of her breasts brush against the hair-roughened muscle of his thigh. His erect shaft prodded at her hip.

"You're completely in my hands now, Lana." He trailed his fingers along her spine until he found the swell of her behind. "You like that idea?"

More than he knew. It wasn't only her body she wanted to give him, but her absolute trust. The unreserved love she'd always felt. "I'm all yours." It was true in every way imaginable.

"You got that right." He slapped her across the cheeks and she bucked from shock. The sensation of pleasure-pain shot straight to her core, making it quiver before traveling up and tightening her nipples where they brushed against his leg. "I can do whatever I like with you when you're like this. Naked, bound and helpless."

His words fired her arousal. He gave her another spank, as restrained as the last one. The sting teased her, made her wetter. Lana arched her spine, thrusting out her ass in a blatant invitation that Brody accepted by peppering her cheeks with soft beatings that tantalized nerve endings she didn't know she had. Lana found herself gyrating wildly against the reined force of his hand, advancing to meet each spank instead of shying away.

"God you're sexy." He buried two broad fingers inside her with a pillaging thrust. She tried to widen her stance but the rope at her ankles prevented it. "Wet and desperate for my cock."

Lana pushed back against his hand, wanting him to fill her harder, wider, deeper. Wanting his cock so much it brought tears to her eyes. She couldn't do anything in her position other than take only as much as he would give her, when he wanted to give it.

"I could make you do anything right now, Lana. Force you to take me any way I want. Here," he said and pumped his fingers harder inside her slick channel. "Or here, in this lush mouth of yours." He traced the outline of her lips with his free hand. Lana clutched him between her lips and drew him in, sucking his finger to indicate how much she'd enjoy sucking his dick.

Brody thrust that finger in and out of her mouth, as though he too was thinking of forcing her to service his erection. "You're trying to make me lose it. You're not in charge here, honey, I am."

Withdrawing his fingers from her pussy, he brought the flat of his hand down on her again, and this time he unleashed more of his power. Lana gasped as the sound of flesh on flesh echoed off the walls of the cabin. Brody stilled his movements immediately. "Are you all right? Was that too—?"

"Don't stop!" Lana yelled, cutting him off. "Make me take it, Brody. I want it harder." She circled her hips. "I've been sooo bad. Make me pay for it."

"*Jesus.*" He rasped the word, then took her where she wanted to go, beating her ass with his broad, callused hand until Lana was screaming from the sheer blinding ecstasy of it. She felt a sharp jolt each time his hand marked her, every time her breasts rubbed over his leg, the pain coupled with an even stronger rise of pleasure. The rope at her wrists and ankles added fuel to the fire of her arousal, making it seem like he really was forcing her to submit to his whims, that she wouldn't be allowed or able to refuse any request. She considered herself an independent person and was shocked at how feverishly aroused relying so completely on him for her pleasure made her feel.

Disappointment filled her when he rose, leaving her alone on the bed. But that feeling soon gave way to excited anticipation when she heard the clink of metal on metal. A belt buckle.

He came to stand beside her. Reaching under her body, he took a breast in his hand and squeezed lightly. Lana arched into the touch, the action curving her spine and thrusting her backside upward. "You have been bad, Lana. Opening your legs over and over again for a nasty brute like me. And you loved every minute of it. Every time I fucked you, you only wanted more."

It was true. She had an insatiable hunger for Brody's particular brand of loving—forceful and conquering, tempered by moments of tender generosity that made her heart clutch. He ran the belt softly over her flesh, already heated from his hands, before threading it between her legs and rubbing the soft leather over the slick folds of her sex.

Unable to speak, Lana rocked against the too-slow motion he set. When he drew the belt away, she moaned a weakened protest. "You loved it when I took you standing up in the shower," he remarked, his voice a thick husk. "Didn't you?"

Without further warning he brought the strip of leather down across her cheeks. Lana gasped. The slash of pain ran a distant second to the spike of excitement that shot to her nipples. Her thighs quivered, her knees were so weak she wasn't sure they could support her any longer. Fortunately Brody was right there, holding her upright with his free hand.

He brought the belt down again. "Didn't you?"

Lana found her voice at last. "Yes."

"And you loved it every time I went down on you, ate your sweet pussy."

"Yes." She'd especially loved that. She'd had no clue before, the things a skilled man could do with his tongue.

The leather flashed across her ass again. "And that time I came over and you opened the door to me dressed in nothing but a lacy white night gown that I could see right through." He caressed the sting out of her skin with a soothing touch as he recited the example. "I wanted you so bad I had to bend you over the couch and have you right there. I didn't even have to ask nicely. You just opened up and let me in, let me pump in you until you were gasping and begging me to make you come."

He ran his finger along the heated slit between her cheeks, stopping short of invading her flesh as she wanted him to. Lana thrust her hips at him, but he denied her. "Do it again now, honey." His voice was a mere thread, and Lana heard the note of desperation underpinning it. He had her at a distinct disadvantage and, as he'd said, could make her do anything he wanted. But his words were as much a plea as a demand. "Beg for me."

"Please, Brody. Please, please, please. I can't take it anymore." She didn't care that she sounded broken and frantic. She only wanted him to take her over the edge of reason as he had so many times before. She'd had no idea it was possible to need an orgasm more than she needed her next breath. "I need you so much."

Easing his thumb into her aching emptiness, he reached his middle finger up and over her clit, rubbing it in a circular motion that made her erupt instantly against his hand. Impossible to stop herself clamping her thighs together, hard, trapping him inside as her pussy went into spasms.

"Oh, sweetness, you came." Her muscles quivered around him, sucking at his continued penetration. "But only a small one. Do it again for me."

He plunged his fingers in and out of her while she

responded to the rhythm. Almost at once she came again, crying out in relief as the waves crashed over her.

Exhausted, she slumped on her bound hands, hanging her head between her shoulders. She was dimly aware of the snap of latex, of Brody's movements as he settled behind her. His words were punctuated by panting breaths. "Lie down flat. Stretch out for me."

She did as he instructed, wondering how he was going to work his way inside her when her legs were clamped together. Gripping her ass, he pulled her folds far enough apart that the tip of his cock could probe her entrance. When he began to push inside, Lana gasped. The space was so tight, her canal made narrower by the position of her legs. He had to move in slowly, each inch he advanced forcing her flesh to give way to accept him.

It was exquisite. On the one hand she felt powerless, not even being able to spread herself open and invite his entrance. On the other she knew by the astonished, grateful words he whispered that this way clamped his shaft tighter than ever before. Lana glowed from the inside out, amazed at the innumerable methods her body could employ to bring him pleasure. She wasn't without power; she held an equal share of it.

When he was settled inside her from base to tip, Brody lay on top of her, his chest to her back, his weight supported on his elbows. He nibbled at her earlobe as he began to thrust, each glide of his cock making Lana moan. She'd already climaxed twice, but this position was so erotic. Her breasts ached where they were pressed into the bed, and her clitoris still throbbed with the need for further attention. Knowing she couldn't do anything about it without Brody's help made the arousal more intense. "Brody, I have to come again."

"Oh God, sweetness, you're unstoppable." He sank his teeth lightly into her neck. "You need me to help?"

Lana groaned. "You know I do."

Bracing himself on one elbow, Brody slipped a hand beneath her body, sliding it over her breasts and stomach before finally touching her pulsing lips. He found her engorged nub and stroked it expertly.

"Yes." Lana thrust into his touch as much as she could as he thrust inside her.

His movements became hurried, frenzied as he touched her, fucked her. "Hurry, baby. I'm going to lose it."

He pounded inside her, barreling home with desperate plunges that satisfied her as nothing else could. She yelled out her orgasm just as the harsh rasp of his breathing turned to a groan of bliss and he emptied inside her.

Long moments later Lana was still shaking. She felt the answering tremors coursing through Brody's frame as he eased out of her and onto his side. They lay together in a heap of exhausted, shell-shocked repletion.

After a while, Brody moved. He started untying her. "Are you okay?"

She was so far beyond okay she needed a new word to describe how she felt. "I am *so* fine." She rolled onto her back, her legs and arms now free.

He chuckled at her weary enthusiasm and, with a tenderness that made her ache, brushed her hair back from her face. "I thought I might have gone overboard, but you...sweet mother of God, you're perfect." He brushed his lips over hers. "Simply perfect."

The soft kiss deepened, became something more passionate that reached down into Lana's soul and curled warm fingers around it. She lay still while Brody kissed away the last thin protective shield from her heart. She'd never understood that sharing your body with a man wasn't the same as giving yourself to him. She understood the differentiation now. Right or wrong, smart or not, she belonged to Brody, heart, mind and soul.

If she lost him now, a part of her would die without him.

He rubbed at the skin of her wrists, which was tinged lightly pink. Lana could only imagine what color her ass was.

"How did you know I wanted to do that?" Brody asked. "Did Sidney tell you?"

Lana's heart stopped flat out as the implication of his words penetrated. "W-What?"

He winced and Lana knew she hadn't misinterpreted what he'd just unwittingly revealed. She sat up, instinctively grasping at the edge of the bed sheet and trying to cover herself with it. Suddenly her nakedness seemed absurdly inappropriate. What had moments ago been a warm fuzzy ache in her chest grew cold and hard. "You've slept with Sidney?"

Chapter Twelve

"It's not what you think."

Wasn't that the oldest line in the book? "She just happens to know what you're into in bed? Oh God." Lana covered her mouth on a gasp. What about Drew? Everyone at the Grill knew Sidney and Drew had been an item since the first night they met. If Brody and Sidney had been together it must have been since then. "Brody, how could you?"

She went to scramble off the bed, clamoring to escape the swamping feeling of sickness. Lana didn't know what was worse—the discovery that Brody's scruples weren't as ironclad as she'd always believed or the understanding that she hadn't blazed a new trail with her little naughty-girl performance. He'd already been there, done that. With his best friend's girlfriend. Correction: his best friend's *wife.*

He grabbed her before she made it off the mattress, snaking an arm around her waist and pulling her back against him. "Lana, listen to me, it wasn't like that. Drew knew about it. It was his idea."

She scoffed. "That doesn't make any sense. You...you cheated."

"No. I'd never do that." He said it with such conviction that Lana stilled. "It was what Sidney wanted. Both of us at the same time."

Comprehension settled into the silence. Why she should feel embarrassed, Lana had no idea, but her entire body blushed crimson. "Oh."

"I thought she must have told you. I have no idea what women talk about with each other."

"We're friends, but not *that* close. Why would you think she told me something so personal?"

"I thought you were jealous today when you saw me hugging her." His voice lowered. "And you came here wanting to be spanked."

She hadn't been embarrassed about that until now. "Believe it or not I thought of that all by myself. To think I felt like some wildly adventurous vixen and all along..." She wasn't surprised Brody had spanked women before, but she had never expected to find out he'd done it with someone she knew. She felt cheated, and not nearly as seductive as she had a few moments ago. She released a bitter laugh. "I guess I'm not so special after all."

He made a gruff sound and tightened his arms around her. "Don't say that. You're more special than you know."

"Right."

"Do you have any idea how it excites me that you came here off your own bat, wanting exactly what I wanted?" He turned her around in his arms, forcing her to face him. His smile was full of amazement and, Lana dared to hope, affection. "You're a bloody thrill a minute, Lana Green."

She felt herself melting. A more silver-tongued man might have employed a thesaurus full of words designed to enchant. Lana figured she'd take *a bloody thrill a minute* over that any day.

Boy, Lana, you're so easy. "You don't have feelings for Sidney?" Petite, beautiful and gregarious, Lana always had thought Drew's wife was more Brody's type than she herself ever could be.

"I thought so once but nah. One time with me and she couldn't wait to run back to Drew. We're just friends—I promise." He grinned. "So there was no need to look like you were going to scratch her eyes out today."

So she *had* been completely transparent. She pursed her lips. "If you think I'm going to get into some bikini-clad bitch fight with another woman over you so you can watch, you've got another think coming."

"Oh shut up, will ya? I told you that was a one-time deal." He flipped her back on the bed and covered her with his body. "I like it one on one."

Her flesh responded eagerly to his words and the seductive kiss that followed. She felt drowsy but utterly rejuvenated in the confidence stakes. "So you don't want me to play at being the filling in a man sandwich?"

His look was lethally unimpressed. "No. Where do you get this language?"

"The Internet. Because thinking on an objective level I have to say"—she pretended to picture it, letting out a low whistle— "lucky Sidney."

"Don't go getting any ideas. I'm finding I'm a lot more possessive than Drew."

Lana felt giddy because he was possessive of her. She'd told him not to act this way but he couldn't help himself. "Are you sure? Because if Jake Gyllenhaal's available, maybe I could be persuaded."

"Jake *who*?"

From his thunderous expression, Lana deduced Brody had no idea who she was talking about. "He's a movie star, Brody.

You can't go kick his butt." Reaching up she smoothed the frown lines from between his eyebrows. "You really leave civilization behind when you go away, don't you?"

"Pretty much. I head into port when I have to, for supplies or to visit old friends."

She paused. "Women friends?"

"Sometimes." His lips executed a rueful quirk. "Not this last time."

"Why not?"

"I don't know." He lifted a shoulder dismissively and Lana felt sure he was going to change the subject. But he surprised her by elaborating. "The thing with Sidney was weird. It was wrong because she wasn't mine, but on some level it felt right too. I guess I wanted something like that, only without the wrong part. To be with someone I liked and respected, to have something that wasn't...empty."

And then she'd come along, offering a meaningless fling, treating him like some stud thoroughbred, and he'd fallen back into an old pattern he'd been trying to change. Even though she knew it was the only way he would have entered into an affair with her, Lana experienced a sweep of regret. She didn't want to be one of those empty flings he referred to. She couldn't be another one of the women friends he called on when it suited him. It would have to be all or nothing.

The thought of *nothing* was too horrific to contemplate, so Lana kept her focus unwaveringly on the possibility of *all*.

"Hey, Lana." He cupped her face in his big hands and his expression was painted with sincerity. "I don't feel that way about what's going on here. It's not empty. I like you. God knows I respect the hell out of you."

For now Lana decided that was more than enough. His words warmed her, made her feel like she was glowing from the inside out. "Ditto to you."

He appeared uncomfortable with the implied praise. His cheeks colored as he dipped his head and began nibbling on her neck. Sighing, Lana tilted her head back and let him taste her, feeling the slow burn of desire simmer inside as he started playing lazily with her breasts.

Abruptly, he lifted his head and frowned. "You're not thinking about that Jake guy are you? Because I haven't heard it's an actual law that you can't kick a movie star's ass."

Brody jealous of a man she couldn't get in a million years was so deliciously amusing that Lana burst out laughing. Even dared to tease him a little. "Actually I'm thinking about both of you. Me sandwiched between you and Jake. He did play that gay cowboy, so there's some nice imagery."

"Honey, I do *not* play that way."

She'd never doubted it. If it was possible for a man to be more than one hundred percent heterosexual, Brody was the prime example. "It's my fantasy—you do what *I* want."

"Why did I ask?" He growled the question in irritation. "You're going to use that now aren't you? To get yourself all revved up when you're *entertaining* yourself."

"I will *now*. Thanks for the idea."

"Christ, woman. Shut up and kiss me."

Lana was only too happy to oblige, knowing that while Brody Nash was around, not even Hollywood heartthrobs stood a chance.

Morning came.

Brody watched the slowly rising sunlight play over the contours of Lana's back, the soft ridges of her spine a strand of pearls buried beneath the pale sheen of her skin. He didn't want to wake her, but he couldn't resist tracing his fingers over that very feminine curve, softly brushing over each bump and indent until he reached the place where the sheet covered the swell of her ass.

He lifted the sheet. A rosy blush tinged her flesh where he'd laid his hand on her last night, and where the belt had licked at her skin. Brody remembered vividly the way she'd succumbed eagerly to the bondage, how she'd writhed and begged for every spank, and he grew uncomfortably hot and hard. Maybe he didn't care so much if he did wake her, he thought as his erection bumped against her hip.

Brody sensed the moment she woke by the way her body tensed beneath his hand. He could tell she was holding her breath and, with that strange understanding he'd begun to develop, identified the maelstrom of emotions churning her thoughts. It was after dawn, the first time they'd woken in the same bed. Somehow he knew she was wondering if she should have snuck out before sunrise, the way he had after each night they'd spent together.

Looking back on that shamed him. Lana deserved better than to wake alone, wondering if he gave a damn about her at all. "Breathe, Lana. You'll do yourself some damage."

She let the air out of her lungs. Her voice was husky from sleep, her greeting timid. "Ah... Hi. How long have you been awake?"

"A while."

"Oh. Do you want me to...?"

Leave. His mind filled in the blank with the certainty of ink. Feeling lower than a snake's belly for making her think she'd done the wrong thing simply by falling asleep, Brody pulled her tight against him. It was hard to get the words past the restriction in his throat. "I like waking up with you."

She sagged into his embrace and Brody felt the relief coming off her like a tidal wave. Then she let out a soft chuckle and wiggled her bottom against his hard-on. "You really, *really* like it?"

Brody smiled. "Insatiable wench."

"I am, aren't I?"

Instead of being chagrined, she seemed enormously proud of the fact. Something inside his chest did tumble turns. As he rolled her onto her back and slid on top of her, he decided it must be the rush of lust pumping his blood around his body. He refused to believe it was his heart falling over.

Burying his face in her neck, he uttered the invitation before he could think about how unwise it might be. "I'm going to take the boat out. Spend the day with me."

"I don't know how to sail."

"Since when has inexperience ever stopped you from doing anything?"

She grinned and wriggled beneath him, the slip-slide of her body under his adding strength to the erection pressing against her stomach. "You have a point."

"It's more than a point, sweetness." He moved her thighs apart, delighting in the way she compliantly wrapped her long legs around him. "Are you going to come with me or not?"

"Yes." She pressed her pelvis into his and smiled devilishly. "And yes."

He laughed. "I've created a monster."

"I've got news for you—I existed long before you deigned to sleep with me."

And she would exist long after they were over. She'd move on and utilize all her newfound skills and appetites on another man, a more suitable man. Pretty soon Lana was bound to tire

Sami Lee

of the limits inherent in their affair.

But she wasn't tired yet. Right now, her silken heat beckoned him, welcomed him without resistance and trapped him inside the walls of heaven. *Live in the moment, Nash. Take what you can get while you can.*

He kissed her, slow and deep as he sank into her body in languorous repetition. She met the dance of his tongue, the rock of his hips, her body arching and undulating to the rhythm that drove him. He listened to the harsh rasp of her breathing and knew it would be easy to make her shatter around him, knew the ripple of her muscles in the throes of orgasm would draw the tension out of his body in the mind-numbing response he couldn't help but keep coming back for.

"Brody, we can't."

The distress in her voice made him still. "Are you sore?"

"No, but you're not wearing anything."

His heart gasped to a stop as her meaning sank in. *Jesus.* Stopping to deal with protection had completely slipped his mind.

Not once had he risked a pregnancy. Years ago, he'd sworn off the idea of ever having kids. He couldn't be sure of his child-rearing abilities, and he'd cut off his own arm before he'd be as inadequate as his own parents had been. So the momentary temptation that swept through him, that told him with Lana it was worth the risk, should have scared the shit out of him. But the idea of getting Lana pregnant was neither terrifying nor repugnant. A voice whispered in his head, insidious and frightening.

If she was going to have your baby, she wouldn't be able to leave you.

It was the strangest thought he'd ever had. He ought to know better than anyone that mothers sometimes left their
176

children.

"Brody, I want to, but—"

"I know, we can't." Under the circumstances he was stunned by how difficult it was to pull out of her. Rolling onto his back he stared up at the ceiling, trying to calm the rapid thump of his heart.

When she propped on her elbow and laid her hand on his chest, his pulse rate only increased under the soft pressure of her touch. She trailed her fingers down over his stomach, edging closer to the place where he was still hot and hard. Trapping her wrist in his hand, he halted her progress. "Don't."

He realized he'd been too gruff when she blanched and snatched her hand away. "Okay."

Fighting the urge to reach for her and pull her back to him, Brody got out of bed and pulled on a pair of board shorts instead. "I'm out of condoms." And apparently he couldn't be trusted to do the sensible thing right now.

"Brody, you're the one who taught me loads of things you can do without going all the way."

Her sassy expression did nothing to deflate his erection. She was on her haunches on the bed, the sheet a soft tangle around her knees. Brody remembered the first time she'd been here and how she'd shyly tried to hide her body, had actually apologized for it. Now she sat before him, naked and unashamed, so sexy she made his head spin, and he thought, *I did this.* He'd had a hand in bringing out Lana's inner siren, had helped her feel like the beautiful woman she was. He'd actually given her something, instead of only taking, and never in his life had he felt so damn clever.

The heady realization had him ripping off his shorts ten times quicker than he'd put them on. To hell with it. Perhaps he couldn't be trusted but Lana could. She always seemed to keep focused on the fact their affair was all about sexual exploration.

He climbed on the bed on his knees, facing her. He traced a hand over her stomach, dipping it downward to thread through her curls. "Do you know what the sixty-nine position is?"

She grinned. "Yes."

From the Internet he supposed. He should have known. "Do you want to try it?"

Her grin widened and her eyes flashed with enthusiasm. "That sounds like fun."

Brody chuckled. "*You're* fun," he countered, enjoying the burst of her laughter as he wrestled her to the bed. "More fun than I've ever had."

As long as it was still fun, why ruin it? Brody thought and tumbled into the sweet heat that was Lana.

Lana's spirits were still buoyed hours later when the *Sunset* cleaved the rippling waters of the bay, the spring breeze lending power to the mainsheet and mitigating the heat of the sun. Brody insisted it was safer for her to remain in the cockpit with him while the boat was in motion, and he explained what he was doing every time he adjusted the sails or changed tack. He even let her steer, and when she sang an old song about sailing the high seas, Brody laughed at her antics and kissed her neck.

They came across a pod of dolphins around midday, and Lana watched in awe as they leapt and danced through the water, looking very much like they were showing off. Lana felt their actions expressed her own sense of elation.

The sensible voice in her head told her not to let her hopes run away with her, but Lana was no more capable of preventing joy from expanding in her chest than she was of stopping the wind from blowing. It was a perfect day and she was with the man she loved. Curbing her exhilaration was impossible. Neither was she sure she wanted to hold back her emotions any longer. Brody's attempt to end things had been a dismal failure because her love was stronger than his fear of commitment. Why not let it flow freely?

Eventually she lost sight of the playful mammals and shortly afterward Brody anchored just offshore of a tiny island. "Lunch time. Are you hungry?"

Lana grinned. "Aren't I always?"

Chuckling, he planted a kiss on her forehead before slipping below deck. A short time later they were eating fresh sourdough bread with thick cut slices of ham and Swiss cheese. Brody had bought the supplies while Lana had raced home to grab her bikini and a few other essentials. She wondered if Brody had also thought to pick up a pack of condoms while they were separated.

If not, it didn't matter. Lana had brought a few from her drawer at home and she had every intention of using them. It occurred to her she should probably go on the pill, if this thing with Brody was going to continue. If she had anything to say about it, it would continue for a long, long time. Lana couldn't prevent a smile from playing with her lips.

"What are you thinking about?"

Her smile widened. If only he knew. "You."

He cocked an eyebrow and flexed the muscles of his chest. "You want a piece of this?"

Did she ever. He looked like the rugged model from some cologne ad with his jaw shadowed and chambray shirt hanging open, the sun glinting off the dark strands of his hair. Lana let him see the way her gaze trailed over him. "Oh, I want the whole thing."

Something cooled in his eyes, and Lana wondered if he guessed she was talking about more than his body. Hoping to cover the slip, Lana spoke hastily. "See, you have corrupted me. All I can think about is sex. Whatever did I do before you came along?"

His face eased into a smile. "I don't know. What do you do when you're not with me?"

I think about when I'm next going to be with you. God, she was obsessed. "When I'm not on the computer I like to read and watch movies." Lana winced. "Gosh that sounds boring. But I'm not really much for socializing. Told you I was a nerd."

"Socializing is very overrated." His gaze swept over her. "And if you're a nerd, then I think they're very *under*rated."

The way he was looking at her made her heart flutter and rise. "You're good for me."

His forehead scrunched. "How do you figure that?"

Lana shrugged. "I have fun with you. You make me feel special."

"You are special. You don't need me to make you feel that way."

His tone was defensive, as though he was offended by her compliments. "Is it so terrible to contemplate the possibility someone might think well of you, Brody? That someone—that I—might need you?"

He was silent for a long moment, his gaze on her face. Then he moved toward her on his hands and knees, stalking her like a lithe jungle cat. His arms bracketed her body as he hovered over her, his closeness activating her nerve endings. He slid his hungry gaze over her green and white striped bikini. "I know what you need, Lana."

He began at her throat, trailing kisses over the tender flesh and gradually moving downward until he found the swell of her breast. Lana quivered in response, even as she knew he was using sex to avoid a discussion that had become dangerously close to meaningful. When he shifted the material of her swimsuit aside and closed his mouth over her nipple, Lana rose into the soft caress, wanting him to recognize that she was giving more than her body. Once again she offered her heart.

Right there on the deck with the sun high overhead and the seagulls flying in curious circles above them, Brody kissed his way all over her body until he reached the juncture of her thighs and gave her an orgasm he didn't make her beg or even ask for. He gave and gave until she touched the clouds. Afterward, when she lay flat out and panting with satisfaction, Brody moved back up her body and looked down into her face. "You're beautiful."

Touched by his sincerity, Lana whispered, "When I'm with you I do feel beautiful."

He smiled slowly, tenderness etching lines around his eyes. "Good."

Lifting a hand, she trailed it down his strong cheek. Her heart was so full it felt close to bursting and for once she wanted him to see it, no matter how risky it was. Before she could come to her senses she let the truth out. "I love you."

She braced herself, waiting for anger or a sardonic joke. The moment passed in silence. At last he turned his face into her hand and sighed her name into her palm. Then he sat up. "I think I'd better take you home."

Lana watched, blinking in puzzlement, as he rose to his feet. "You're really going to pretend I didn't just say I loved you?" Her voice shook. She wasn't sure if it was from anger or fear.

He threw her a look over his shoulder. It was so detached, so remote that Lana shivered. "No," he said. "I can't do that."

As he strode back to the cockpit, Lana's stomach turned. She hadn't felt the least bit seasick all day, but now she could easily have hurled her lunch into the ocean. A sense of foreboding hovered over her like a black cloud, even though the sky was ceaselessly blue.

She watched Brody trim the sails with a pained heart and felt her dreams ripping away on the wind as the boat moved toward land.

A little over half an hour later, Brody walked her along the dock to the marina car park, where she'd left her scooter. "I had a really nice day." She hated the desperate thread in her voice, the forced small talk. But she had to get him to discuss what happened somehow.

"Me too. I've had a good time with you."

His use of the past tense seemed preternaturally loud in the deserted parking lot. That sick feeling rose again and Lana swallowed bile. "Brody, about what I said on the boat—"

"Lana..."

"Just pretend I didn't say it. I didn't..." She couldn't bring herself to say she hadn't meant it. "All I want to do is have fun with you, like we agreed last night."

"I didn't agree to anything."

Lana's steps faltered as they neared the Bee Wee. "But... We..."

He stopped her with a hand on her arm. His touch slid down until it encircled her wrist. "I don't want to drag this out any more than I already have. I realize I've led you on and I didn't want to do that."

"Led me on?" He had no clue what he was saying. He wanted her. The way they'd made love last night and the day they'd spent today... He had feelings for her. She knew it.

"I should never have messed around with you in the first place. It was bound to get complicated."

"Wait, back up a minute." Lana shook her head. "I got into this. I started messing with you, remember? I've consented to all the subsequent messing."

"Lana." He stared into her eyes at last. The bleakness she saw in his gaze scared her. "You think you love me."

"I don't *think* anything. I do love you." The disquiet became a roaring tempest inside, making it impossible to halt the rush of admissions. "I've always loved you, have hoped for so long you'd catch up, that you'd one day have feelings for me too. I can wait as long as it takes, but I can't pretend anymore that I don't have these emotions. I think we belong together."

He appeared stricken by her confession. "Oh Jesus, sweetness, I had no idea. I would never have touched you if I knew you felt that way."

"Don't you think I know that?" She spat the question. "Why do you think I made up all that rubbish about wanting to use you for sex practice? You're not a warm-up, Brody, you're the main event. I don't want anyone else. I want *you*."

He swore softly. Turning away, he scrubbed a hand down his face. At length he said, "I'm not the guy you think I am. You thinking you love me... It's crazy, Lana. You don't even know me."

"Whose fault is that? You don't talk to me about anything, not about your childhood or your future. Nothing that *matters*."

"There's nothing to talk about. My mother left when I was

eight. She couldn't handle the fact that I needed her to be a grown-up. My dad blamed me for her desertion. At least I figured from the way he started smacking me around."

"Oh, Brody..."

"Don't do that. Don't feel sorry for me. Just try to understand. I'm not like other people—people like Drew, who expect things are going to work out for them because they always have. Things don't work out for me. I've accepted that. I won't accept it for you. You can do better."

"Better than you?" Lana shook her head. "You don't know what you're talking about."

"I can't be the guy you need, Lana. It's not in me."

"You can do anything you want to do."

"I don't *want* to do this. I don't want to get married or have kids..."

"You think I do?" Lana interrupted him. "I'm twenty-three. I don't want children yet."

"But you will, one day. You need someone else, someone who can give you that. I like my life just the way it is and I'm not about to change it. You'd be wasting your time with me. There's no future to talk about, not for us."

His stark words seeped through her like an oil slick, smothering the last glistening rays of promise. Lana didn't want to let go of them, but the darkness moved through her heart, inescapable. He wasn't merely saying he wasn't ready, or that he didn't love her. He was saying he never would, that he didn't *want* to. There was no hope.

No hope.

Her throat closed over. She had no idea what she could say anyway. She stared at her hand, realized he was holding it close to his chest. The contact mocked her and she wrenched free of his grasp. How could he destroy her dreams like this and still want to hold her hand?

"I'm sorry, Lana."

"You're sorry." Her voice sounded flat, mechanical. "What are you sorry for? That you had anything to do with me in the first place, or that I'm not woman enough for you to love me?"

"*What?*" he rasped, clearly shocked. "Lana, you're more woman than I can handle. Even now part of me wants to drag you back on the boat and keep you there. Go at it until neither of us can even lift a limb, let alone fuck."

She flinched at his choice of language. With crushing devastation, Lana realized the extent of her foolishness. All along she'd been making love but Brody had merely been fucking. Even last night when she'd given him everything. She'd thrown her heart into the mix but he'd only been playing games.

Seeing her reaction, Brody framed her face with his hands so she had to meet the wealth of regret in his eyes. "But sex, no matter how good or intense it is, isn't love, sweetness. I'm the first lover you've ever had and you're confused. You'll see that in time. But right now, I can't keep letting you think this thing between us is going somewhere I can't take it."

He was killing her. Somehow she had to get out of here, to make her legs work. She didn't want to hear another word confirming the awful truth, that all she'd ever been to him was a convenient body. It was beyond mortifying. She couldn't believe she'd told him how she felt. Was he secretly laughing at her?

No, it was worse. He felt sorry for her. Pathetic, lovesick Lana Green had made herself the object of his sympathy.

Holding herself together with a mammoth effort, Lana stepped back, evading his touch. She fumbled with the catch on her motorcycle helmet. Putting all her concentration into that one, minor task, she at last managed to unclasp the strap and slip the helmet on her head. She spoke in surprisingly even tones, as though she were hearing her voice on an answering machine, a disembodied imitation. "I'm sure you're right. I'm probably just confused. The sex has been very..." *heartstopping, breath-stealing, wonderful. So amazingly wonderful,* "...nice. You must think I'm very silly."

His voice was husky. "I don't think you're silly."

She stepped onto the Yamaha and fit the key in the ignition. How she did it without fumbling when her insides felt like they were shaking apart, she had no idea.

"Lana, I really wish..."

She turned over the engine, drowning out his voice. She didn't think she could take any more of his forced kindness. Brody being nice because he thought she was fragile. She didn't want him to know how he'd shattered her. She glanced at him and forced herself to smile, trying to appear normal, *whole.* It felt so strange.

His mouth was moving in speech, his brow furrowing. She read his lips. *Be careful.*

She almost laughed. For a moment she considered running him over with the scooter he hated so much. How dare he express concern for her welfare when he'd just ripped out her heart?

But if she voiced her anger, she'd cry too. She knew it. It was as though tears filled her veins, diluted her blood. It made her feel light, empty. Her hand trembled on the throttle.

She only had to make it ten minutes and she'd be home, away from him and this humiliation, the gaping sense of loss.

She turned the scooter and headed out of the parking lot without once glancing back.

Chapter Thirteen

The jarring ring of the phone started again.

Lana ignored it like she had the other times. She pulled the pillow tighter around her head, longing for the temporary succor of sleep to claim her once again, to provide a momentary relief from the pain. Her dreams were of him, because she always woke with tears on her cheeks. But she couldn't remember them. The blankness of slumber was her only saving grace.

The next time she woke someone was pounding on her door. She stuck her fingers in her ears, willing whoever it was to go away. Probably her neighbor. She should really get up, go tell the old lady she was all right. But she wasn't all right and neither was she ready to put on a believable façade. So she stayed where she was and begged for unconsciousness.

Some time later the bed wobbled. Comprehension came slowly. Someone had their hand on her arm, shaking her. "Lana, wake up. It's Sidney. Your neighbor let me in. Are you all right?"

"G'way," she muttered. Her voice rasped, her throat raw from crying.

"When you didn't turn up at work last night we were worried." By we Lana knew she meant herself and Drew. Not Brody. "It's not like you to ditch a shift without calling. Are you sick?"

"Just tired. Need sleep."

Sidney tugged the pillow from her weak grasp. Pushing her tangled hair back from her face, the other woman took one look at her and sighed. "Oh no. It's Brody, isn't it?"

Hearing his name out loud had the tears rushing back. They tumbled from her eyes and onto the sheets. Her body shook with racking sobs. She didn't fight it when Sidney pulled her into an embrace and started rocking her back and forth.

She was helpless to stop it all spilling out, the whole sorry story. "He doesn't—want me. Won't even—try..." She shook her head and hiccupped. "Why won't he even try to love me?"

"Because he's a complete moron," Sidney said crossly. She held Lana while she cried for what seemed like hours, while she wailed out her pain and frustration, admitted how long she'd carried a torch for a man who didn't want to love her. Who thought she should go find somebody else. Somebody else! There would never be anybody else, not like him. She'd never love anyone again the way she loved him.

When she was cried out, Sidney made her a cup of tea. Lana took a sip but it tasted bitter and unappealing. She put the cup back in the saucer.

Sidney asked, "Have you eaten?"

Lana shook her head. "I feel like I'm going to be sick."

"I'll bring you something light from the restaurant. You need to eat."

She didn't want to eat. She wanted to starve until she faded away to nothing. Dimly Lana recognized how disturbing the thought was. Perhaps that's how a person died of a broken heart. She had to pull herself together. "You don't have to wait on me. I promise I'll eat."

"I'll bring food anyway. Forget about your shifts for a few days, we'll get someone to cover."

Lana hadn't even thought about work. "Oh, Sidney. I'm not sure I can..." She held a hand to her mouth. She didn't think she could ever go back to the Grill.

Sidney seemed to understand. "We'll work something out. If it comes to that, we'll find you another job. It's the least we can do. Brody's our friend. I feel responsible somehow."

Sidney's mention of her relationship to Brody reminded Lana of what he'd told her on the boat. "He told me about the two of you. Or I should say the three of you."

"Oh." Sidney's cheeks grew pink and she looked away. "I'm surprised he mentioned it."

"I always used to figure that maybe if I was more like you he would have..." She toyed with a strand of her hair. Her voice turned bitter. "Maybe I should have dyed my hair blonde instead."

"Don't you dare say that. You can't change yourself into something you think he wants—especially when he doesn't even know what that is."

"He knows what he wants all right. Me out of his life."

"If that's true he doesn't know what's good for him. I knew there was something wrong when I saw him last night. He was standing right in front of me but it was like he wasn't even there, like he'd slipped away when I wasn't looking. I can't believe he wants to be this unhappy." Sidney squeezed her shoulders. "You really threw your heart at him, didn't you?"

"I had to give it my best shot." In years to come, when she didn't feel too wretched to see a silver lining to the situation, she'd at least be able to say she'd done that. Lana hoped it would bring her some comfort.

Sidney smiled sadly. "I wish Brody had done the same, honey. I really do."

The other woman left and Lana forced herself to take a shower. She choked down a few stale crackers and some orange juice. Then she went back to bed for another twelve hours.

The following day when there was a knock on the door, Lana went to answer it. Mick looked her up and down, taking in her wrinkled T-shirt and faded running shorts. "Sidney said you were feeling poorly, but this is ridiculous."

When she smiled this time, it didn't feel quite so horrible. She accepted the chicken potpie he'd brought her for lunch and forced herself to eat almost half of it. She even managed to keep from crying until he was gone. He was under the impression she had the flu, and Lana was thankful for Sidney's discretion. She didn't want it get back to Brody that she was a blithering mess.

The next day lunch was delivered by Courtney, who gave her a sympathetic look that had Lana slipping backward into self-pitying tears. "You were right, Courtney," she wailed. "I should have listened to you."

"No, you were right. I was too bitter. I didn't realize what I was passing up."

Lana looked at her, glad of the diversion from her despair. "You and Mick?"

Courtney's cheeks colored. "I didn't want to say anything because you're so miserable, but we went for a drink that night he asked me to and, well, he hasn't left my place since."

"Oh, Courtney. I'm so pleased for you." With fierce determination, Lana squashed the kernel of envy. She didn't want to be that petty because she'd made a mistake.

"Thanks. I think this might actually work out. As long as he doesn't wise up and realize he doesn't want to be with me after all."

Her tone was jovial but Lana sensed the real fear beneath Courtney's words. She looked at the young woman's glossy dark hair, creamy skin and piercing green eyes and saw a beautiful person most men would kill to spend time with. Instead Courtney was wondering what Mick saw in her.

Why did women beat themselves up like this? Why had *she* for all those years defined herself by the results of her interactions with the opposite sex? She was her own person. A smart, likable, valuable person who ought to know better than to think herself unworthy of anyone.

She had been worthy of Brody, it was he who'd made the mistake. They could have been so good together, but he'd chosen not to take a risk. That wasn't her fault—it was his. The knowledge brought her some relief from her own self-recriminations, while it fuelled the latent anger that had been too crowded out by the pain to grow.

Over the course of the next few days, that anger gave her strength, while each visit from the staff of the Grill improved her general disposition. One by one they came, bringing food and funny stories in an obvious attempt to cheer her up. Lana realized how lucky she was. She had friends and people who cared about her. It was only Brody who didn't want to be a part of her life.

Sidney's fabrication about her having the flu allowed her to hold on to a modicum of pride. It was pride that brought about her decision. Five days after that scene in the marina car park, Lana resolved to go back to work.

Whatever it cost her, she would bury her emotions. She would not cry in front of Brody Nash. She would not cry *over him,* not anymore. She would not let him chase her out of a job she was good at, that she enjoyed.

She had to get on with her life without him.

For a week, Brody felt like death warmed up tepid. Barely alive, riddled with disinterest and a sense of apathy that was way too familiar. Then Lana walked into the restaurant.

It was like having his chest slammed with a pair of those electric paddles from a medical-drama show. He'd thought she would quit, that he'd never see her again. The prospect had hollowed him out, yet also filled him with a cowardly relief. Hollow was easier to deal with than this needy sense of desperation, of euphoria mingled with nausea.

Why did she have to be so resilient, so classy that she could walk through those doors with her head held proud and her eyes clear and bright, as though he'd never hurt her? Why couldn't she have slunk away like he'd thought she would—like *he* had?

He stood there like a dolt as she strolled into the kitchen and said a cheery hello to the guys. She smiled and looked radiant and perky and so over him. She didn't shy away but stared him dead in the eye. "Hi, Brody."

He opened his mouth but nothing came out. Before he knew it she'd left to start her shift out front and he was still standing there doing an impression of a fairground clown.

Drew let out a low whistle, sending him a look that read *you gave her up, moron.*

Brody worked through the rest of his shift, so distracted by Lana's presence he burned his knuckles on a griddle pan, spilled a pot of béarnaise sauce and almost chopped off his left thumb. Eventually Drew told him to go home because he was a danger to himself and others.

Home—what a joke. He didn't have a home. He lived on a floating mausoleum. He spent his time in abject solitude, working toward what purpose? The truth was he had no goals, no direction in life. His boat wasn't a home. It was the place that kept him separated from other people, a distinct, isolated entity. He wasn't living a life. He existed in some state of limbo between his past and the dark mystery of his future, not moving forward or back, floating in a sea of nothingness.

Dead calm.

Once upon a time if he'd felt this bad he would have headed down to O'Ryan's, tied one on and picked a fight, more in order to do himself some damage than to hurt anyone else. But he hadn't touched a drop of alcohol since that night on the boat because Lana's words were still stuck in his mind. *Is this how you deal with things you don't want to face?*

He didn't want to be his father—didn't have to be if he made that choice. So he went to the Buchanans' house instead, where he let himself in and crashed in the guest room. In the morning he made blueberry pancakes for Ray and Carol before starting on a batch of chocolate cupcakes because he knew how much Carol liked them.

Lana had liked them too, he recalled, and his grip on the wooden spoon grew tight. He turned and found Drew's mother watching him, her blue eyes tinged with sadness. No doubt Drew had told her everything. They'd always been close. "Don't you look at me like that too. I'm sick of everyone thinking I'm a big fat idiot."

Carol's brows hiked. "Do *you* think you're an idiot?"

Yes. "I'm the only one who's using his brain."

"What about your heart, Brody? How's it faring?"

So fucking poorly I can barely breathe. "Just dandy.

Couldn't be better."

"My gosh you're a stubborn boy."

"I'm not a kid anymore, Mrs. B."

"Then why is it every time I look at you I still see that terrified, sullen child who deserved so much better than he was handed in life?"

"I don't know. Maybe you need glasses." The stupid comment made him think of Lana, and he got so riled he raised his voice at Mrs. Buchanan, something he'd never done. "When are you going to stop treating me like some kind of bloody hero because I happened along when Drew needed a hand? You think I dove in to save him that day because I gave a shit about him? I jumped in because I didn't give much thought to my own life, not because I thought his was so bloody priceless. I figured maybe I'd die instead of him and that would have been fine with me. I'm no hero."

Carol regarded him in silence across the homey, cluttered kitchen. At length she said, "But you didn't die. When do you suppose you're going to do something about that?"

Brody pushed out a frustrated sigh. "I live just fine." *No you don't, you exist.* "I like my life." *You're miserable and lonely.* "There's nothing wrong with being alone." *Maybe not, but how's it working for you lately?*

Like he said, he'd dived into that flooding drain all those years ago only because he couldn't care less whether he lived or died. He'd never realized that sense of apathy hadn't really gone away until recently. Until Lana had made him yearn for things he never knew he needed.

He sank with a thud into a dining chair and dropped his head into his hands. He thought of all the years he'd spent at this table, invited to dinner by little more than a twist of fate. The Buchanans had shown him mealtime could be a raucous, joyful affair and not merely a cold can of spaghetti taken from the stash under his bed. He'd always hidden stuff there on grocery day, before the end of the week came around and his Dad had drunk all the money, leaving nothing for food.

When he'd become a chef he'd thought, *This is it, the best thing I can do with my life.* To turn the generosity the Buchanans had extended to him into a skill that gave others enjoyment was more than he'd ever hoped to achieve. To ask for anything else would have been greedy.

Now, he did want more. He wanted Lana.

Warm weight came to rest on his head, Mrs. B stroking his hair. The gesture was so motherly that Brody's heart contracted. He realized she was right—he hadn't come very far since he was eight. He was still stuck in the past, as deprived as that kid who'd so badly needed his parents' love.

"Some people aren't built to raise children," Carol said. "Unfortunately, Larry and Francine fell into that category. That was their failure, not yours. They didn't do right by you, but that doesn't mean you don't deserve to be happy."

Knowing that logically and hearing Carol say it with such unqualified certainty were two different things. His throat felt tight, and Brody was seriously afraid he was going to cry. Even so, he spoke over the constriction. He knew Carol would hear the emotion in his voice, yet he spilled out a truth he should have admitted long ago, because this woman who'd taken him into her heart deserved to know what that meant to him. "I used to wish you were my mother."

"Oh, sweetie." She looped her arms around his neck and hugged him tight, pressing her face into his hair. "I thought I was."

His shoulders shook as the tears slipped out, embarrassing him, making him whole.

It was a long time before either of them spoke. Birds twittered in the trees. The radio played softly in the background, a song about the one that got away. Eventually, Brody got a hold of himself, and Carol broke the silence. "So tell me what you're going to do about this girl you love."

Instinct told him to deny it but the words died in his throat. Realization hit him like a rogue wave. The heart palpitations, night sweats, that stabbing pain that assailed him when he let himself actually think about the reality that he'd lost her—no, pushed her away. It all added up to one thing: he was in love with Lana. Those weeks with her had imbued his life with vibrant color, and now everywhere he looked all he saw was gray.

All he'd ever see was a monochrome world if he couldn't have Lana.

"Oh Jesus." He scrubbed a hand down his face, trying to dispel the seasick feeling. The room still tilted, like when a squall hit at sea and it was difficult to get a bead on the horizon. The enormity of his stupidity made him dizzy. He'd had her right there—in his arms, in his life—and he'd as much told her to grow up and get over him.

He could have had everything with her, there could have been a *them*. He could have shared himself with her like she'd wanted him to. He was beginning to get the feeling she would have accepted him, warts, old wounds and all. That maybe she was the only person who had ever really gotten him, and loved him anyway.

But what had he done? Pushed her away because it was easier than waiting for her to do the job for him. It hurt too damn much to be rejected. In the process of saving himself, all he'd done was hurt her. He was a selfish, worthless pile of dirt who didn't deserve to walk in Lana's shadow. And Mrs.

Buchanan thought he could do something to fix that?

Forget it.

His gut clenched. He felt like the dumbest man on the planet. "I really fucked up." He turned to find Drew's mother's brows arching and muttered, "Sorry, Mrs. B."

"I'll excuse you as long as you promise you'll tell her how you feel."

"I can't. She won't listen and I don't blame her. It's too late."

"There's no such thing as too late."

Her conviction made his pulse pick up speed. He'd come to accept over the years that the Buchanan matriarch was usually right about everything. Was it possible she was right about this?

He thought of Lana, of everything she would want eventually. Commitment, family, the life he'd told himself he could never have because he wouldn't know how to get it, let alone keep it. Then he thought of the years spent here at the Buchanans' house and realized he did know how a real, healthy family functioned. He had examples to draw from, experience that could outweigh genetics and bad memories.

That *would* outweigh those things, if he decided to make sure of it.

The Buchanans had always treated him as one of their own, but deep inside he'd known he was on the fringes. He couldn't accept that anymore. It wasn't enough to be on the outside, he wanted in. He wanted something real with someone like Lana.

No. Not someone *like* Lana. It had to be her. The woman he admired and adored, who made him laugh and burn hot. The one person who'd taken away the loneliness, who had let him

Sami Lee

into her heart. The only woman he'd ever loved.

"I don't know what to do," he admitted. He wasn't sure he'd been truly honest with a single person until this morning. How could he ever be enough man for a special woman like Lana? "I need help. I can't do this on my own."

She squeezed his shoulders. "Sweetie, you have to. Whatever you need to say, it has to come from you. After all"— she patted him on the back as she rose to her feet—"it's your fuck-up."

"*Mrs. B!*"

She winked at him. "You're not the only one who can curse like a sailor, Brody—*I* use a filter. Now, you go get that girl."

Go get her. Easier said than done. "What if..." Brody swallowed panic, its taste bitter in his mouth. "What if she doesn't want me anymore?"

"She might not. But you have to decide if Lana's worth the risk."

"She's worth it."

Mrs. Buchanan appeared satisfied with his unequivocal statement. "I thought as much."

After breakfast Brody headed back to the boat. Cruising down Main Street on autopilot, he racked his brain for ideas. Women liked flowers, right? He could fill Lana's flat with them, hundreds of blossoms in an array of bright hues. On second thought, all of them should be purple, he knew it was her favorite color.

He could hire a limo, take her to dinner at a fancy restaurant. Immediately he scratched the idea. Lana wouldn't be impressed by that. She was the kind of woman who was happy eating French toast at the kitchen counter, who laughed when he nibbled the crumbs from her lips.

A wave of grief swept over him. How could he have been so stupid?

Applying the brakes at the crossing, Brody let an elderly lady traverse the street at snail's pace while he stared out the window. His heart stopped when he caught sight of Lana emerging from the independent grocers, a calico bag in each hand. The bags looked heavy and he had to fight the urge to run over there and take the burden from her. As he stared she glanced his way, as though she'd sensed his scrutiny. Her steps faltered and she tripped on a crack in the sidewalk.

Brody opened his door, ready to bolt over there and catch her, pick her up and bundle her in his car. Take her away and tell her he loved her, fix everything as best he could.

A car horn reminded him he was idling in the middle of the road, and he realized the old lady had moved on. Lana recovered her balance and hurried down the footpath, not looking back. Dismissing him, just as she'd done last night at the restaurant. What she was apparently planning to do from here on in.

Shoving the car into gear he drove on. Flowers and dinner wasn't going to cut it. Telling her how much he missed her wasn't going to achieve a damn thing. She wouldn't let him get past hello.

By the time he parked his car in the marina lot, Brody knew what he had to do. He was going to have to tell her everything, the most painful, humiliating things. It was the only way to make her understand why he'd done what he had, why he'd been too afraid to give them a chance.

There was no guarantee she'd be willing to listen. He'd already used up his share of second chances. But he had to try. He had to show her what he was willing to do. He couldn't leave a single stone unturned. He had to give her what was left of his heart and hope she was willing to accept it.

This time it was his turn to beg.

Chapter Fourteen

"Hi, Lana."

Lana glanced up from where she was stashing her bike helmet in the cupboard to see Brody standing at the end of the bar, watching her. Her heart gave that sickening kick it always did, and she went through her now-familiar struggle to appear composed and unaffected. Completely unaffected. "Hello. I see we have a lot of people booked in for tonight. It should be busy." *That's it, Lana, keep it professional.*

"Yeah. I guess word has gotten out that we have the prettiest waitresses on the east coast."

She was halfway to standing when the impact of his words hit her. Her heel caught on the edge of the rubber matting behind the bar and she tripped. She saw Brody step forward as though to catch her and knew there was no way in the world she could keep an emotionless persona if he touched her. Her arms cartwheeled and she teetered backward, crashing into the open door of the dishwasher and scratching her leg.

Glancing down, she saw a run in her stocking and swore a streak of a particularly vulgar cobalt blue.

"Are you okay there, potty mouth?"

Lana shot her gaze toward him. His lips curved in a half smile and there was something squishy soft about the way his eyes held hers. Her insides turned to toasted marshmallow in response.

It had been all she could do the last few days to get through each shift with her mascara intact, and Brody had been keeping a respectful distance. There was no way she was going to hold it together if he looked at her like that.

"I have to go put on my spare pair of stockings." She practically squeaked the explanation, turning away in a rush before his eyes could pull her in.

He was nice to her all that night. Making friendly chitchat, being frighteningly agreeable when she brought a meal back to be replaced because she had totally stuffed up the order. His sweet smile and these-things-happen attitude had her scratching her head. But that was nothing next to her shock when Drew interjected, "He won't be so blasé about a wasted steak when he's an owner instead of on salary." At Lana's perplexed look Drew elucidated, "He's finally taking up my offer to become a partner."

She could only stand there mutely, slowly going deaf from the ringing in her ears as Brody informed her, "Drew has this idea of expanding, buying that little café downtown and turning it into a wine bar. Thought I might run things here while he's busy becoming a business mogul."

"But...but that'll mean..." *You can't keep taking off every six months to God knows where. You'll be committed.*

He caught her gaze. "The *Sunset's* not going anywhere for a while."

Lana's felt like she was having a coronary. Why Brody's decision should affect her one way or another, she didn't know. It didn't change things between them. All it meant was there was absolutely no relief in sight. The relentless agony of pretending she wasn't utterly heartbroken would go on and on and on because Brody wasn't leaving.

She was going to have to move to Uzbekistan.

The night passed in a blur. Lana messed up three more orders and spilled a glass of wine in a customer's lap. When Sidney suggested she clock off, Lana was only too relieved to accept. She raced out to the parking lot and straddled her scooter.

"Maybe you shouldn't be riding that thing."

She glanced up and saw Brody approaching. Fury spiked inside her. Didn't he realize what seeing him did to her? "I'm not interested in your opinion, Brody."

"It's not an opinion, it's a concern. You seem a little distracted and I don't want you to get hurt."

He didn't want her to get *hurt*? Oh that was rich, coming from him.

"I've got my car here tonight," he cajoled. "Why don't I give you a lift home?"

"Aren't you needed inside? You being Drew's *partner* and all?"

"The rush is over, he can do without me."

"And you're such an expert at working out when people can do without you."

She turned the key in the ignition but Brody reached out and grabbed the handlebars, glowering at her. "Calm down, Lana. You're going to have an accident."

Didn't he know that if she took a spill in the main street at high speed it couldn't possibly hurt worse than looking at him? She found herself with a dearth of witty parting lines so she settled for vulgarity. "Fuck off and leave me alone!"

She roared the engine and backed away with a spray of gravel. She flew out of the parking lot, leaning on the throttle and wishing she rode a Harley. This thing just didn't have enough power to put the required distance between her and Brody at the speed with which she required it.

How dare he act like he gave a damn about her? And flirting with her too, that stupid comment about pretty waitresses. Didn't he know he couldn't say things like that? They were so far beyond idle flirting it wasn't funny.

And where did he get off making promises to Drew he wouldn't keep? Brody no more wanted to settle down and be a business owner than she wanted to ride her scooter off a cliff. He didn't do responsibility or commitment. He'd proven that time and time again.

Lana pulled the scooter into her carport and shut off the engine. After the harried ride home, it took her a moment to get used to the stillness. Her fingers trembled because for the first time since she'd gone back to work she'd actually had to deal with Brody face to face, instead of pasting on a fake smile and tiptoeing around him.

She hadn't done a very good job of it.

"What the *fuck* did you think you were doing?"

Whirling around, she saw Brody storming through the gate with such force it snapped back against the fence, making the row of pickets shake. "What am *I* doing?" She glanced down the street and saw his car parked under a streetlight. "Did you chase me?"

"Someone had to look out for you. You were riding like a fucking lunatic."

"This thing"—Lana waved her arms at the scooter—"only goes the speed of a ride on lawn mower. How much damage could I have done?"

"There are other cars on the road, Lana. Someone could have sideswiped you. You might have ended up in the hospital."

"And that would have been your problem how?"

In the glow from the porch light she'd left on, she saw his dark eyes do that soft thing again and his voice dropped to a husky murmur. "How do you think?"

She had no earthly idea. She couldn't have recited her two times tables with him standing so close. Lana stepped back and folded her arms across her chest. "I'm at home now and as you can see I'm in one piece." *Sort of.* "I'd like you to go."

"Can I..." He glanced down at his feet. To Lana's amazement he shuffled them like a nervous kid. When he looked up again the raw need in his eyes twisted her heart. "Can I come in for a minute?"

The blood drained from her face. "My God. Is this some kind of...booty call?"

He blanched. "No. I only want to talk."

Lana shook her head. "We never talk. *You* don't talk."

"I want to now."

"It's *too late.*" Lana was powerless to halt the downward slide into hysteria. "I want you to leave. What's wrong with you? Don't you care about me at all?"

"Of course I do." He put his hands on her shoulders. "That's what I want to talk to you about—about us."

Lana tried to twist away from him but she couldn't escape. He was too strong and he held her with a gentle but sure grip. It terrified her how badly she wanted to step into him and ask him to hug her. Fear made her lash out. She peppered his chest with her fists. "There is no us. You told me that and I didn't want to believe it. Well, you showed me, Brody. I believe you now, so go *away.*" She shoved against him but he was harder to move than a Sherman tank. She tasted the salt of her tears and knew she'd lost her battle to keep from crying in front of him.

There was nothing left. Even her pride was gone.

"Please, don't do this to me," she implored. "Don't you know how hard it is to even look at you when you don't...when you don't..."

His fingers curled tighter around her shoulders. "When I don't what?" he rasped.

"When you don't...love me." The words spilled out on the back of a sob that shook her body so hard her knees buckled. She sagged like dead weight as the tears rained out of her. Unable to support herself, she had no choice but to allow it when Brody pulled her up against him and enfolded her in his arms.

She cried against his shirt, knowing how ludicrous it was to stand in the arms of the very man who had shattered her and let him offer comfort. But she took her perverse sustenance from the way his hands rubbed circles over her back, from the way he held her so tightly against him, as though he were afraid to let her go. From the words he whispered in husky apology. "I'm so sorry, baby. I thought I had things the right way round but I didn't. Lana, I do love you. I do."

A wail tore from her throat. Having dreamed of hearing those words for so long, she thought she must have imagined them, that she was becoming delusional. She pushed against him but was too weak to combat the way his arms banded around her. "Lana, listen to me. I love you." He cupped her face in one of his hands and tilted it so she was looking at him, facing the intensity in his dark gaze. "I *love* you."

The taut passion in his voice made her breath stop in her throat. The cool night breeze brushed over her face, the heat of his chest warmed her palms. She knew she wasn't hallucinating, but the moment seemed surreal, halfway between dream and reality. Two weeks ago if he'd made a declaration like this she would have been overjoyed. But a fortnight of crying herself to sleep every night had taken its toll. She felt numb and shell-shocked, not nearly ready to trust what she was hearing. "I don't understand," she choked. "You told me we had nothing together, no future..."

"I shouldn't have pushed you away after that day on the boat. I said a lot of things that hurt you and I regret that so much. But at the time I thought I was doing you a favor."

"How could you think that?" This time when she levered away from his chest he let her go. Her voice trembled. "You broke my heart, Brody."

A pained look marked his features. "Lana, I broke mine too."

"Why? Why would you do that? All I wanted was to love you but you wouldn't let me. You didn't want me."

"That's not true. I wanted to keep you with me so bad I started to lose my mind. I even thought about getting you pregnant that morning on the boat, because I knew that would tie you to me. I knew I'd do something to hurt you if I didn't let you go. I figured I had to do it."

"*Pregnant?* You told me you didn't want children."

"Hell, I didn't know what I wanted that day. I knew I was losing you and it was tearing me up."

"You didn't lose me, Brody." Lana enunciated her words very carefully, not certain he fully understood how greatly his actions had impacted her. "That implies it was my choice to leave. You threw me away, and that was so much worse. You think you were torn up? I felt like I'd been hit by a truck. I gave you my heart and you discarded it because you were afraid I'd hurt *you*. Don't pretend you did it for my benefit."

Weakened by the outpouring of emotion, Lana let the wobble in her legs take her down. She sank to her knees on the grass, her hands shaking. An instant later Brody was kneeling on the lawn before her, taking one of her trembling hands tightly in his. "You're right, Lana. I was a coward. I've been afraid for a long time."

"Of what?" Lana pushed her free hand to her chest. "Of me?"

"Of the kind of thing we have together. Of love. Of hope. Of reaching for something I didn't think I was capable of holding on to. Rejection is...hard for me."

The anger seethed within her again, granting her renewed energy. She yanked her hand from his grasp. "You think it wasn't hard for me? To hear you blithely dismiss my love as some kind of adolescent crush I'd get over? Your rejection cut through me like a machete. You don't have the market on pain cornered, Brody."

"I know. God, I'll do anything if you tell me there's a chance you'll forgive me. Would you, Lana? Could you ever see yourself giving me another chance?"

The moon shone down, a large silver orb that illuminated the desperation in his expression. Tearing her gaze away from the sight, Lana looked up to the sky. She realized the moon was full. It had been a month since the night of Sidney and Drew's wedding. Four weeks in time, an eon in emotional distance. She wasn't that same girl anymore, the one who was so cavalier with her heart.

She loved Brody, and figured she probably always would. But she wasn't so blindly sure being with him was right for her anymore. She answered honestly. "I don't know."

Chapter Fifteen

Brody's heart sank to the pit of his stomach. It was too late. She'd already decided he was a lost cause. He couldn't blame her. It was exactly what he'd tried to convince her of all along, exactly what he'd always believed.

"I'm sorry." Her voice was thick with regret. Even after all he'd done, it wasn't in Lana to be hurtful for the sake of it, and the goodness of her spirit humbled him, made him love her even more. "But you can't erase everything that's happened with a few words, Brody. Even those words."

"You're right. Words don't mean anything." What had he been thinking, coming here with nothing more to offer than a clumsy declaration of love?

Hopelessness threatened to engulf him. He experienced the familiar urge to run, to get the hell away from this place and disappear into the wide blue, where he could be alone. To lick his wounds. To get over Lana.

In a moment of clarity that dispersed the fog in his mind, Brody realized Lana wasn't so easy to get over. He'd never forget her, would never find anyone like her again. He knew it as surely as he knew the dark after sunset never did last forever—there was always light approaching.

Focusing on that light, he knew it would only get closer if he cast the dark demons from his mind. A thread of steely determination entered his voice as he felt his resolve harden. He couldn't give up yet. "Lana, I want to tell you a story. I need you to listen for a little longer. Will you do that much for me?"

His heart pounded as she stared at him. What if she told him to go? His resolve didn't shift. "If you tell me to leave I'll just come back tomorrow, and the next day and the next, until you give me a chance. It's your call, but I'm warning you I'm not giving up."

Into the silence, she sighed. "You can come in, but only for a minute."

Brody latched onto that thread of hope like a life buoy tossed into a stormy sea. A minute was a start. When she went to rise to her feet Brody stood and helped her up. He took heart from the fact she didn't shake off his touch as they walked to her door.

Inside, the welcoming warmth of Lana's cozy apartment curled around him, and he knew without a doubt this was where he was meant to be. Despite the crazy clutter and the purple curtains and the explosion of feminine accoutrements, Brody knew he belonged here. Sharing the same space as Lana, wherever that may be.

He would fight with his dying breath for this—for them. The knowledge gripped him, and as Lana stepped into the living room he shot out a hand and curved it over her shoulder, needing so badly to hold on to her.

"When I was eight my mother left me." The words spilled from his tongue, surprising him. Freeing him. Immediately he knew this was what he needed to tell her more than anything else. The only way he could turn the darkness to light. "My father thought she left him but deep down I knew the truth, that I was the one who drove her away. I was there the day she left. Crying in the driveway like my life was ending because I needed so badly for her to be a mum, to stay and fight for me, no matter how hard it was for her. But she didn't want to fight. You know the last words she ever said to me? 'I love you, kid, but I can't do this anymore. I never asked to be a mother.' Well, I never asked to be her kid either, but I couldn't change it. I couldn't run away from it, no matter how hard I tried."

Lana was listening to every word he said, he could sense the tension in the way she held her breath. He was glad she didn't turn around. Brody couldn't look at her, not while he told her this. He felt too exposed, too damned afraid she too would see whatever it was his parents had seen. The thing that had made him so unlovable. "Dad had never hit me before, so to be fair to my mother she might not have known what she was really doing when she left me with him. And as for my father... I don't know. I think he actually loved her, and her abandonment was his excuse to be bitter for the rest of his life. All I thought was, if this is love I don't want any part of it.

"Life seemed so much easier that way. I don't rely on anyone and no one relies on me. No love to warp things. Everything free and easy and above all, no expectations. I didn't realize how dull and colorless that life was until you showed me. I had no idea how empty I was inside until you filled me up."

She tried to turn but he stopped her by hauling her up against his chest. He knew she would be able to feel the erratic thump of his heart against her back, the restless tempo of his breathing, but he didn't want to hide the depth of his emotions from her anymore. "I do love you, Lana. I'll say it as many times as it takes for you to believe me. I was weak and stupid, and I'm sorry. Whatever you need, name it and it's yours. Buying into the restaurant was only the beginning. I'll sell the *Sunset* too, if you want. I'm not going anywhere without you."

"I don't want you to sell the boat." The shock was clear in

her voice. "You love sailing."

"The *Sunset's* my escape hatch." He spoke his next words with steady sincerity. "I don't need it anymore, because I'm not running from you—never again."

"I don't want you to sell it. I don't want you to change into something you're not for my sake." She squirmed against him until he felt compelled to release her, hoping against hope it wasn't the last time he got to hold her in his arms. She turned to him, her eyes blazing. "Is that the only reason you bought into the restaurant—to prove yourself to me? Because if that's so we're back to square one. You'll grow to feel trapped and blame me."

"I'd never feel trapped—I want to be with you. Haven't you heard a thing I've said?"

"I've heard you all right. I've heard you admit that on some level you had me in the same category as your parents. What did you think—at the first sign of trouble I'd abandon you? Or worse—deliberately harm you? I'd never do *anything* to hurt you. How could you not know that about me? I've loved you since the first moment I saw you. As nuts as it sounds, I've always believed I was destined to love you. Walking away was never on my agenda."

"Is it now?" Terror made his mouth arid. "You do still love me, don't you, Lana?"

A split second's warning was all he had. Not enough to evade her fist as it shot out, driving into the centre of his chest and knocking the breath from his lungs. "Of course I still love you! That's not the issue. I need to trust you not to balk anytime you start thinking you're not good enough for me. That's what this is all about isn't it? Your parents were horrible. So horrible I could..." Her jaw clenched and her fist tightened.

After a moment she carried on, sounding a little calmer but

no less impassioned. "I wish I could erase all that happened to you, but I can't. I can only assure you that I never, not for one minute, thought you were in any way inadequate. You're more than enough for me, just as you are. But if you can't see that..." She shook her head. "I can't love you halfway, Brody. If you're not in this one hundred and fifty percent, I can't risk letting you in again. It hurt too much to lose you the first time."

"Lana, I'm in this all the way." He let the conviction ring clear in his voice. "I've been so miserable without you, utterly lost. I can't go through that again either. I'm tired of keeping my distance. I want to be close to you. I want to make love to you every night and wake up beside you every morning. I want to know all your secrets, your hopes, your dreams, and I intend to give you mine in return. I do have dreams. I'm learning to let myself have them, and they all involve you. But you're wrong, sweetness—I'm not enough just as I am. Any fool can see you're too good for me. I'm still a work in progress. But one thing I promise is I'll never go backward from here. I want to move forward, with you. Always with you."

"Oh, Brody." Her voice softened and his heart turned over. "All this time you were afraid I'd walk away from you, when I thought you would turn around one day and realize..."

"Realize what?" he rasped into the pause.

"That *you* could do better." She hiccupped a sound somewhere between laughter and tears. She tugged on her ponytail. "Look at me. The red dye's all gone. I couldn't be bothered with it, just like I can't be bothered putting on makeup lately or wearing those cleavage-creating wonder bras. This is me." She ran her hands over her body then threw them up in the air. "I'm mousy and plain when I don't do all that girlie maintenance I've been doing. Are you really sure this is what you want?"

He'd never been surer of anything in his life. Brody stared at her, unable to fathom that the breathtaking female standing before him still had such insecurities. That steely sense of doggedness settled into a hot throb of determination that breathed fire into his body. He could feel it burning in his eyes as he stepped toward her, backing her into the wall. Felt it in his groin as he caught the fresh, potent scent of her. "You think I give a damn about hair color and makeup? Dye your hair purple for all I care. If you never wear a bra again, I'd be a happy man. Get a tattoo if you want, preferably something small and sexy, right here." Grabbing her ass cheek he gave it a possessive squeeze. "Where I can see it every time we get naked.

"Do whatever you want, you'll still be the woman I fell in love with. The one who danced like a wild creature in the middle of an empty restaurant. She made me so hot I had to take notice. She carried herself with such integrity and honesty that I learned to respect her. One night, she stormed onto my boat and made me face what a louse I'd been because cowering isn't in her nature, and I admired her so much I thought there was no way I'd ever be worthy of her."

Whatever it took, Brody vowed that he *would* be worthy of this love that had come out of the background and changed him. It had saved him when he hadn't even known he was drowning. He owed his life, everything he was and would ever be to Lana, his sweetness, and he was going to spend the rest of his days repaying her for what she'd given him.

He reached up and touched her face, tracing the line of her cheekbone, her lips. When she puckered up and kissed his fingertips, he lost his breath. "I'm not sure when I fell in love, Lana. It could have been at any one of those moments. In fact, I don't know why they call it falling, because I feel like I've risen up to it. I love you, sweetness. Let me show you how much. Let me make love to you—*now*, before I die from wanting you."

The only movement Lana felt capable of was a small nod of assent. Her heart had expanded in her chest, emancipated at last by the powerful beauty of his words, so plainly and honestly spoken. He meant them with every fiber of his being. Lana could see the truth in the glittering heat of his dark gaze and the taut desperation lining his face. He really, really loved her. And what was more, she actually believed his love matched her own.

She felt lighter than air as Brody lifted her in his arms and carried her to the bedroom, where he lay her on the bed with such sweet tenderness that dampness slipped from the corner of her eye. Brody used a thumb to wipe it away. His gaze brimmed with such unadulterated love that a laugh of happy delirium burst through her tears. Lana put her hands on his face and pulled him down for a kiss that sealed their future. She felt the promise of it seep into her bones and shape her into a new, fuller person.

They undressed each other with soft impatience, stripping away the final layers of fear with their clothing. When they lay side by side, naked, Brody's hot gaze trailed over her. He ran his hands over the lines of her body with a reverent touch, staring at her so long Lana began to tremble beneath his scrutiny. "You..." he began, placing a soft kiss to the skin just below her navel, "...are so..." he moved up her body until he nuzzled her breast, the fine abrasion of his stubble beading her nipple, "... beautiful."

Sighing, he took her peaked flesh into his mouth. Lana cried out at the exquisite relief of it, of once again knowing the intense pleasure she'd thought lost to her forever. The perfection of being this intimate with Brody, the man she loved with all her heart. He had made her feel this way before—beautiful, desirable, feminine. Amidst the misery of the last two weeks, all she'd been able to focus on was the opportunities he'd denied them. She'd forgotten what he'd already given her.

Never again. From now on she would be this woman, his woman, always. Twining her fingers through his hair she arched into his mouth, whispering his name like a prayer as he worshipped her body, laving and gently sucking each breast in turn until Lana's whimpers became impatient and needy. Then he slipped down her body and bathed her most secret places with his tongue, all the while whispering praise for how gorgeous she was, how sweet, how loved. In moments her climax burst into his mouth, a wild offering that he tasted with a long, husky moan.

Afterward he moved up her body, bracing above her. Lana wanted to return the favor but she could read the need in his eyes. He wanted to be inside her. "Yes," she whispered, as if he'd voiced his intentions. She reached down and took him in her hand, gasping at the solid weight of him. He'd never felt so hot, so swollen, so alive. As she began to stroke him, his member pulsed with the blood pounding through it, his chest heaving with his ragged breaths. "You see what you do to me?" His eyelids fell to half-mast as he covered her hand with his and guided her actions. "*Mousy* and *plain* would not put me in this state, sweetness."

"Oh, Brody." Lana writhed on the bed, the very act of touching him enough to turn the ache of longing into a powerfully desperate craving that had to be fulfilled. "Please, now. I need you now."

He found a condom in her drawer and rolled it on. His fingers trembled on the task and Lana's heart softened, opened further to him when she wouldn't have thought that possible. When he was done she took his hand and linked it through her own, smiling. Then she raised her hips to meet his as he advanced and little by little, as though savoring every exquisite sensation, entered her.

She held his gaze as they lay motionless, joined as one. After a moment Brody husked, "God I love you."

Lana's breath shuddered out of her. "I love you."

He began a rhythm that started slowly, but soon turned hurried and desperate. He held their linked hands to the bed above her as his body moved in coordination with hers. In the midst of the storm he surprised her by rolling onto his back so she found herself above him. He kept their hands linked on the mattress. "I'm all yours, sweetness."

Lana's inner walls pulsed around him. Feeling it, he groaned, grinding his hips into hers. At once Lana resumed the cadence, riding him as he lay beneath her, offering himself.

She stared into his eyes, their gazes locked as inexorably as their bodies, as she rode him toward sweet, heavenly oblivion.

Afterward they clung together in silent awe, panting breaths rushing out to meet each other. Lana settled in to this new, beautiful truth, feeling the fantasies she used to have slip away to be replaced by a far superior reality.

In the most fanciful of her infatuated dreams, Lana had imagined Brody declaring his love by sweeping her into his arms, carrying her off into the sunset, showering her with compliments and flowers and poetry, saving her from her solitary life. Her Lancelot, her knight in shining armor.

Such immature illusions, she now realized. This was better, because this was real. This was Brody opening up and letting her into places he didn't let anyone else go. This was the man she loved being vulnerable to her, giving her his trust, the most difficult and precious thing he had to offer.

He was her knight after all, but stripped of his armor. And this way, she knew, she could save him too.

"I want to do that again."

Brody smiled into Lana's hair. Not five minutes after she'd laid him flat and loved him to within an inch of his life and she was spoiling for round two. God he adored her. "Give me a few minutes."

She giggled and snuggled more closely into his chest. He really liked the way it felt to have her tucked so securely in his arms. This was how he wanted to sleep every night from now on. He wondered if she'd object when his stuff started taking up permanent residence here. He didn't have much, so there was a good chance he could distract her while he was quietly moving in.

Or he could outright ask her to marry him.

"I didn't mean right this second," Lana said as Brody's heart started doing a crazy, nervous dance in his chest. "I meant again as in lots and lots of times. As often as possible. Once a day at a minimum."

"Only once?"

"I said at a minimum."

"So you did." Brody licked his lips but they still felt dry. Marriage. *Marriage.* It sounded so right in his head. He and Lana, together. Forever.

Another moment passed. Then she said, "I think I really like being in control. Perhaps I'll tie you up next time."

"Fat chance." Even as he muttered the words, images danced in his mind, toying with his libido. Lana would look phenomenal in a leather bustier and a black wig. That outfit and the promise of a blow job might just make it worthwhile.

"Oh, you like that." She rubbed her damp pussy against the swelling at the juncture of his thighs. "I'm surprised at you."

"Don't get too many ideas. I'm the one who decides who's going to get tied up around here."

"Tough words, boss man." Her voice turned from teasing to thoughtful. She frowned. "You are the manager now, at the restaurant. I think maybe I should quit."

His heart slammed to his throat. He tilted her face up so he could look in her eyes. "Why?"

"Don't get me wrong. Sleeping with the boss can be a massive turn-on." Her lips quirked. "But after a while it becomes plain unprofessional."

"Lana, be serious. Don't you like working with me?"

Her smile became softly reassuring. "I love it. But I've been thinking a lot about that Internet café I once told you about. Remember?"

"Of course."

"I think maybe it's time for me to do something for myself, build a dream of my own." She stroked his face. "Can you understand that?"

A sigh of relief slipped out of him. "If it's your dream, sweetness, I'll do everything I can to make it happen. Just as long as you're not trying to get away from me."

She laughed. "Not likely."

"Because I'm never letting you go again. You got it? Never ever, ever. I'm dead serious," he said when she chuckled. "You might as well clear your schedule for the rest of your life and fill my name on every page. There'll be no other men for you, never again. Any guy who comes near you is going to get his ass kicked."

"I see." She propped up on one elbow and stared at him. "You'd better watch out, Brody, that all sounds very permanent."

"So? I'm not afraid of permanent."

She arched a brow. He held her gaze steadily, sensing a challenge in the air. Although he figured the time and place was probably all wrong, he always had been the proverbial bull in a china shop. Besides, he'd already wasted enough time. Now that he'd finally worked out what was good for him, he wasn't going to lose it. He meant every word he said when he told her, "You're going to marry me one day."

She was silent for several painful thumps of his heart during which he wondered if he'd gotten too cocky after all. At last she smiled, slow and sweet and beautiful. "Which day?"

Then she leapt at him and hugged his neck, laughing out loud.

About the Author

Sami's been a secretary, sales assistant, bartender, waitress, student, tutor, human resource manager and administration officer, but at heart she's always been a writer. She enjoys creating emotional, sexy stories about the gorgeous, aggravating men who live in her head and the women who were made to steal them away from her.

Sami lives by the coast in Australia with her husband, two stupendous daughters and a crotchety geriatric dachshund. To learn more about Sami, please visit www.samilee.com. Send an email to sami@samilee.com or visit her blog at http://sami-lee.blogspot.com.

When the sun goes down on their erotic encounter,
who will be left standing?

Chasing Sunset
© 2008 Sami Lee

After an unsettled childhood, Sidney McCall has finally found a home in Graceville. This dream town comes with a dream boyfriend. Drew Buchanan is charming, romantic, completely devoted to her—and he cooks! Now if only the whole commitment thing didn't give her night sweats...

Drew, a professional chef, wants nothing more than to give Sidney everything she's ever dreamed of, both in and out of bed. Even if it means serving up her most secret wish complete with a whipped-cream topping: a tryst with two men. His best friend Brody Nash is the missing ingredient, and the only man he trusts with the woman he loves.

What starts out as a little harmless sexual play quickly boils over into something none of them expected. An emotional minefield that could forever change the course of their lives.

Warning: Contains explicit sex scenes including; ménage a trois, oral sex, stripper heels, creative use of whipped-cream deserts, sex in a public place, light bondage, hanky spanky and hunky, bossy men. In short, more than enough naughty business for one little novella!

Available now in ebook from Samhain Publishing.

hot stuff

Discover Samhain!

THE HOTTEST NEW PUBLISHER ON THE PLANET

Romance, fantasy, mystery, thriller, mainstream and more—Samhain has more selection, hotter authors, and everything's available in both ebook and print.

Pick your favorite, sit back, and enjoy the ride! Hot stuff indeed.

GREAT
CHEAP
FUN

Discover eBooks!
THE FASTEST WAY TO GET THE HOTTEST NAMES

Get your favorite authors on your favorite reader, long before they're out in print! Ebooks from Samhain go wherever you go, and work with whatever you carry—Palm, PDF, Mobi, and more.

Samhain
Publishing Ltd

WWW.SAMHAINPUBLISHING.COM

0619

LaVergne, TN USA
30 September 2010
199115LV00003B/71/P